HOT CHOCOLATE ON THURSDAY

Also by Michiko Aoyama

What You Are Looking For is in the Library
The Healing Hippo of Hinode Park

HOT CHOCOLATE ON THURSDAY

MICHIKO AOYAMA

Translated from the Japanese by E. Madison Shimoda

doubleday

TRANSWORLD PUBLISHERS

UK | USA | Canada | Ireland | Australia
India | New Zealand | South Africa

Transworld is part of the Penguin Random House group of companies
whose addresses can be found at global.penguinrandomhouse.com.

Penguin Random House UK, One Embassy Gardens,
8 Viaduct Gardens, London sw11 7bw

penguin.co.uk

First published in Great Britain in 2026 by Doubleday
an imprint of Transworld Publishers
Original Japanese edition, MOKUYOUBI NI HA COCOA WO, published by
Takarajimasha Inc., Tokyo. All rights reserved.
English-language translation rights arranged with Takarajimasha Inc. through
The English Agency (Japan) Ltd. and New River Literary Ltd.

001

Copyright © Michiko Aoyama 2017
English translation copyright © E. Madison Shimoda 2026

The moral right of the author has been asserted

This book is a work of fiction and, except in the case of historical fact,
any resemblance to actual persons, living or dead, is purely coincidental.

Every effort has been made to obtain the necessary permissions with
reference to copyright material, both illustrative and quoted. We apologize
for any omissions in this respect and will be pleased to make the
appropriate acknowledgements in any future edition.

No part of this book may be used or reproduced in any manner for the
purpose of training artificial intelligence technologies or systems. In accordance
with Article 4(3) of the DSM Directive 2019/790, Penguin Random House
expressly reserves this work from the text and data mining exception.

Typeset in 12/15.5pt Dante MT Std by Six Red Marbles UK, Thetford, Norfolk
Printed and bound in Great Britain by Clays Ltd, Elcograf S.p.A.

The authorized representative in the EEA is Penguin Random House Ireland,
Morrison Chambers, 32 Nassau Street, Dublin d02 yh68.

A CIP catalogue record for this book is available from the British Library

ISBN 9781529950120

Penguin Random House is committed to a sustainable future
for our business, our readers and our planet. This book is made
from Forest Stewardship Council® certified paper.

I

Hot Chocolate on Thursday

Brown

The person I have a crush on is named Ms Hot Chocolate.

I don't know her real name. That's just what I call her.

She always sits by the window in the corner of the Marble Cafe, where I work. She started coming here about six months ago, always choosing the same seat, always ordering the same thing.

'Hot chocolate, please.'

She looks up at me with eyes like dewdrops after rainfall, her shoulder-length chestnut hair swaying.

Marble Cafe is tucked away in the corner of a quiet residential neighbourhood. It's a small place nestled behind large trees, just at the end of a row of cherry blossom trees that line the riverbank. Across the bridge are several stores and businesses, but it's mostly homes on this side, and there's little foot traffic. The cafe doesn't advertise, nor is it featured in magazines. It has managed to keep the lights on, only frequented by those in the know.

Three tables and a counter that sits five. Raw wooden tables and chairs. A lamp that dangles from the ceiling. The cafe is never completely full, but it's never completely empty either. So, every day, I tie my apron strings and welcome customers.

Ms Hot Chocolate always comes in on Thursday. She pushes open our door a little after three o'clock and spends about three hours here. She usually passes her time reading and writing long airmail letters in English, reading English paperbacks, or gazing out of the window. Most of our customers who visit on weekday afternoons tend to be families with children or elderly people; a young woman like Ms Hot Chocolate is a rare sight. She doesn't appear to be a student, and she doesn't wear a wedding band. She's probably a little older than me, and it's been three years since I've had my coming-of-age ceremony at twenty.

I barely know any English. I can't even remember the last time I wrote a letter. So seeing her write about her daily ongoings and feelings to someone in a distant land and receive replies – it feels as if it's all happening in a fantasy world. She writes on stationery as thin as tracing paper and uses envelopes with tricolour borders of red, white and blue. It's

HOT CHOCOLATE ON THURSDAY

mysterious enough that she writes letters by hand in this digital age, but her use of such old-fashioned items makes her seem even more otherworldly. As I pass her table, I catch a glimpse of her writing in beautiful cursive with a fountain pen. I wonder what sort of magic spell she's inscribing.

I truly enjoy watching Ms Hot Chocolate write letters. Her lips form a gentle curve, and a flush of pink warms her pale cheeks. Her eyes are lowered, and every time she blinks, the shadows of her long, dark brown eyelashes dance across the paper.

In these moments, Ms Hot Chocolate never looks at me. That's why I can watch her. I can tell she must genuinely care about the person she's writing to. Warmth and slight jealousy wrestle in my heart.

I started working here two years ago in early summer. It all began with me walking along the river, absent-mindedly wondering just how far the rows of leafy trees stretched.

I was unemployed at the time. Business had faltered at the chain restaurant where I'd worked since graduating from high school, and I'd been laid off. That day, I was walking home from the public employment office, having failed yet again to find a job. I had plenty of two things: worries and time. As I ambled along the river, I let my idleness take over until the rows of trees ended, and there, in the shade of a thicket, I discovered this cafe.

A cafe in a place like this? Before opening its door, I checked the coins in my wallet. I should have enough for a cup of coffee.

Although the cafe was cramped, it had a comforting atmosphere. I felt grateful that it offered me, a person with no place to go, a table. It might have been my first time there, but I felt relief wash over me as if I had returned to my own room. It was the antithesis of the clamorous chaos of the chain restaurant. *If only I could work at a place like this . . .*

My gaze swept across the cafe, and I gasped when I saw a staff member putting up a flyer that read PART-TIME HELP WANTED. *What timing!* My heart was racing as I sat at the counter.

After putting up the flyer, the man brought me a menu and water. He looked about fifty, with a slim build. He had an easy-going face, but the mole in the centre of his forehead was quite striking. I glanced down at the stylish menu, noting the prices before placing my order.

'May I have a coffee?'

HOT CHOCOLATE ON THURSDAY

'Hot, right?'

The man with the mole went behind the counter. I observed him closely as he began preparing coffee with a siphon brewer that emitted a bubbling sound.

'Um . . . are you the manager?'

'Yes, I am. Call me "Maestro". It was my dream to become a coffee-brewing maestro at a cafe.'

The Maestro served me the coffee over the counter. The unglazed cup released a full, strong aroma. I took a sip and found it to be gentle and rich. That single mouthful set my resolve, and I rose from my chair.

'I'd like to work here. Will you please interview me for the part-time position?'

He looked at me with an unreadable face for about five seconds, then said, 'Sure. I'll hire you full-time.'

I stood there with my mouth agape. I hadn't even told him my name.

'But, my résumé and ID . . .'

'No need. The one thing I have is an eye for potential. Would you prefer to work part-time, though? Would a full-time position be a problem?'

'It's not that . . .'

'Then it's settled.'

The Maestro stepped out from behind the counter and peeled the job flyer from the wall.

And just like that, I became an employee of Marble Cafe.

Shortly afterwards, the Maestro told me, 'I'm going away for a bit. You'll have to manage things on your own, Wataru. I was planning on handing the cafe over to someone eventually. I'm glad you arrived sooner than I expected.'

Perturbed, I asked, 'Wait. Didn't you say it was your dream to become a coffee-brewing maestro?'

'Once the dream is fulfilled, it becomes reality. It's the dreaming that I like. So I got what I wanted.'

For the past two years, I've been running Marble Cafe on my own. Of course, the business is still under the Maestro's name; I am the cafe's hired manager. It's practically unthinkable to be suddenly entrusted with running a cafe completely alone, but I wasn't given a moment to question it. There's no employee manual here like at a chain restaurant, and the only thing the Maestro taught me was how to open and lock up.

As I desperately trial-and-errored my way through, I started gaining more regular customers. Among them is an elderly lady who dotes on me like family and a father who often swings by with his child on their way home from kindergarten. Now and then, as if on a whim, the Maestro will glide into the cafe, now thoroughly imbued with my character, to swap out a wall painting or to perch at the counter pretending to be a customer while reading the sports section.

HOT CHOCOLATE ON THURSDAY

My world is confined to this cafe and my rented studio in a two-storey building. Yet, in this small world, I am entirely content. I like my old, cramped apartment with its two-burner gas stove, which is ideal for cooking. More than anything, I love this cafe. And to add to these luxuries, I've even fallen for an intelligent, chestnut-haired customer.

Maybe it's improper for a staff member to have romantic feelings for a customer. But I'm content with unrequited love. As the Maestro said, it's the dreaming that I like. One-sided love isn't so bad. To simply love – that gives me strength and drives me to give my best.

Yes, for instance, on Thursdays, I serve her exceptionally delicious hot chocolate. That's all there is to it.

Mid-July ushers in the end of the rainy season, bright skies.

One Thursday, as three o'clock passes and I begin to feel restless, the door opens as always.

But Ms Hot Chocolate seems different. She's noticeably drained, and her shoulders, from which a tote bag hangs, sag wearily. Unfortunately, her favourite seat has been taken by another customer, a sharp-looking woman in a crisp blouse and pencil skirt. There are several books on her table, and she's intently tapping away on her tablet. Ms Hot Chocolate glances at the woman, then settles down at a free table in the centre of the cafe.

I bring water and the menu to her. Despite it being a sweltering day, she orders her usual hot chocolate, just as I knew she would. Only then does she meet my eyes for an instant before looking back down at the table.

Even after I serve her the hot chocolate, she continues to keep her gaze downcast. She doesn't bring out her stationery or fountain pen, not even a paperback. She just stares at the end of the table.

I see a tear slide down her cheek.

I want to run to her side, but I can't.

To Ms Hot Chocolate, I am nothing more than a button on a beverage vending machine. Judging by her appearance, she must be a well-bred woman, fluent in English, and has lived or frequently travels abroad. The recipient of her airmail correspondence is probably her long-distance lover. She inhabits a faraway world with nothing in common with mine – except for this cafe.

But at this moment, she is close enough for me to

touch her, and if I could, I would like to wipe away her tears, squeeze her hand, and tell her everything will be OK.

But miracles like that do not happen. I don't even really know *what* will be OK. We are cafe staff and patron. The only thing I – a server who can't shed his apron – could possibly offer to Ms Hot Chocolate . . . the only thing . . .

There's a rustle of paper as two books hit the floor. The customer with the tablet sitting in Ms Hot Chocolate's usual seat sighs heavily as she gathers the fallen books. It seems every woman at the cafe today wears a troubled expression.

'Oh my god, look at the time!' She looks up from her watch, then shoves the books into her expensive-looking black bag and hurries to the register.

Perfect! I think immediately, with a pang of guilt. I swiftly settle her cheque and rush to the table with my tray. I gather everything – the glass that held iced coffee, a half-empty water glass, a napkin, a straw wrapper – and place them on my tray. I wipe down the table so swiftly that if there were such a thing as a 'Clean-up Championship', I'd probably win.

'The table's free,' I say, my voice high-pitched from excitement.

Ms Hot Chocolate looks up in surprise. I hesitate for a moment, wondering if I've done something unnecessary. But I want to convey my feelings, so I muster up my courage. 'It's your usual spot,' I say. 'Just being in a place you like can sometimes give you strength.'

Her large eyes widen even more, and she looks back at the recently vacated table.

The next moment, as if the snow has melted away, a smile appears.

'Thank you. You might be right.'

Ms Hot Chocolate moves to her usual table, and she looks out of the window for a while. And when she finishes her cup of hot chocolate, she uncharacteristically orders another one.

As I bring her the second cup of hot chocolate, I see she's begun writing an airmail letter. The moment I'm about to set the cup on the table, she suddenly says, 'Excuse me.'

Startled, my hand falters. A few drops from the shaken cup splatter on to her writing paper.

'I'm so sorry!'

Just when everything is going so well . . . Blood drains from my head to my feet like an ebbing tide. In a panic, I try to wipe the splatters away with a paper napkin.

'Wait!'

Ms Hot Chocolate places her hand on top of mine. My heart flips like a fish out of water.

HOT CHOCOLATE ON THURSDAY

'Look, a hot-chocolate heart!'

Heart?

I look closer, and I see that the hot chocolate has indeed formed a crooked, heart-shaped brown stain.

'How fun! I'm going to send it like this,' says Ms Hot Chocolate, beaming like a child who's discovered a rainbow. I didn't know she could laugh like this. The skipping fish in my chest refuses to calm.

'I'll write "Warm up with some hot chocolate!"' says Ms Hot Chocolate as she pens the words in an elegant, flowing English hand.

She is smiling contentedly in her usual seat.

The soft hands I touched for the first time. The joyful smile meant just for me. I realize that even in this small world, miracles really do happen.

Next to the hot-chocolate heart are the words 'My dear best friend, Mary'. Although my English isn't great, I can read that much. It's a letter to Mary, her closest friend.

I don't know why Ms Hot Chocolate was crying, but I now know that the recipient of her airmail letters is not a long-distance lover. I hide my grin behind my tray.

2

The Earnest Rolled Omelette

Yellow

As I am leaving Marble Cafe, I notice the book sticking out of my bag. The decorative pattern on the cover clashes completely with my Birkin. I shove the book deeper into my bag and head to the kindergarten to pick up my son, Takumi.

Normally, the kindergarten pick-up time is at two in the afternoon, but they offer an extended-hours childcare programme where they'll look after the kids until four o'clock. Thanks to my husband, Teruya, signing us up for this ahead of time, I could attend an afternoon meeting in the office before leaving work early. The meeting ended sooner than anticipated, so I decided to enjoy a cup of tea at my favourite riverside cafe while I strategized for tomorrow.

Marble Cafe is my special hideaway. It sits quietly at the end of a cherry-blossom-tree-lined path, offering a view of the changing seasons through its window.

HOT CHOCOLATE ON THURSDAY

The decor is mellow and soothing, and the young guy who works there is a sight for sore eyes. There's a simple wholesomeness about him that's rare these days. The toasted sandwiches he makes aren't fancy, but they're thoughtfully crafted and have an almost nostalgic taste. A person's character can really come through in their cooking.

But today I couldn't unwind as much. I'd opened my book, ready to dive into an unexplored genre, when I received an urgent email from work. It was a request for help from a team member who'd made a mistake. I quickly issued instructions to my staff and reached out to the client to offer my apologies.

I was focused on drafting an email on my tablet when I knocked my books off the table. One was brand new, but now its corners were bent. I let out a loud sigh. It felt like I'd been doomed to fail.

When I look at my watch, I see it's almost four – time for pick-up. The mid-July heat is still scorching at this hour. It feels like even the sun's urging me to get going, and I hasten my pace as my pantyhose cling to my legs. My bag is bulging with work files and two feature magazines I stuffed inside.

The kindergarten is located across the bridge. First, I'll fetch Takumi, then we'll grab an early dinner at a family-friendly restaurant, head home and then . . . Oh, right, I'll have to give Takumi a bath and put

THE EARNEST ROLLED OMELETTE

him to bed. And I have something I need to practise today, too – something more daunting than work. It's my biggest mission since getting married.

Tomorrow, I have to make Takumi's lunchbox for the first time.

The bento box cookbook I was flipping through earlier at the cafe featured 'Five basic appetizing colours' – red, green, black, brown, yellow. Red is simple: cherry tomatoes. For green, there's broccoli. I'm not confident about boiling it just right, but it shouldn't be too difficult. Nori seaweed for black – I'll make a small rice ball with that. I can fry up mini sausages for brown. I'm not entirely sure how, but I think I can slice them to look like octopi, crabs, or something or other.

Yellow.

Yes, yellow is the problem. When it comes to yellow food, and yellow food for lunchboxes at that, there's only one option.

As the kindergarten gates come into view, it occurs to me that this is my first time picking up Takumi, too. It's been two years since he enrolled, and the only times I've visited the school were for his entrance ceremony, field day and Christmas show. I attended them all with Teruya, always with a video camera in hand. But today, Teruya is not beside me.

As I nervously walk through the gates, I hear

someone greet me with a 'Hello'. When I turn to look, I see four mothers standing in a circle, their children chasing each other around them. I stiffen. I don't recognize any of the mothers or the children. A mum in a striped shirt looks in my direction. Maybe she's the one who called out to me. Her hair is tied back, and silver-rimmed glasses frame her face.

'No Dad today?'

'No, not today.'

I force a polite smile as I rack my brain, struggling to recall who she is. Even though Ms Striped Shirt was the one who approached *me*, she's now grimacing, seemingly unsure of how to keep the conversation going. Anxious to escape them, I bow and turn to the school building. I can feel the other mothers' eyes on me as they smile stiffly and bow.

The moment my back is turned, they start talking.

'Who was that?'

'Takumi's mum.'

'Oh.'

I pause when I hear a clearly disappointed voice from the group say, 'I guess his dad's not coming today. I signed up for extended-hours care today because of my part-time job, and when I saw Takumi was still here, I thought I'd get to see his dad.'

So Takumi's dad is popular, huh? I begin walking again without turning back.

THE EARNEST ROLLED OMELETTE

When I go through to the classroom, Takumi runs up to me, his bowl-cut hair swinging as he yells, 'Mum!' He extends his arms out like airplane wings. Although he's never actually been on a plane, he adores them.

A young teacher follows after Takumi. If I remember correctly, she's the assistant homeroom teacher, Ms Eri. Her skin is smooth like a freshly peeled boiled egg, and she wears a pink apron that suits her perfectly.

'Wow, isn't it the first time Mum's here to pick you up? Lucky you, Takumi!'

That again. Do they all find it so shocking that I'm here for pick-up, or do they just want to see Teruya that much? Maybe I'm being paranoid, but it feels like everyone's silently judging me for not being the one who usually drops off and picks up Takumi.

As Takumi pulls out his schoolbag from his cubby, he turns to his teacher and says proudly, 'Dad is in Kyoto.'

The teacher stoops to meet Takumi's gaze.

'Kyoto? On vacation?'

'Nope, for work!'

'Oh, did your dad start working?'

'It's not quite "work" as you might imagine,' I say as I secure the bag on Takumi's shoulders.

'My house is in To-Kyo, and Dad is in Kyo-To. To-Kyo

and Kyo-To!' Takumi chants as he runs towards the door, seemingly thrilled to have learned a new city name. A five-year-old's brain seems to delight in absorbing new things.

Through the window, I can see the circle of mums, still chatting away.

I whisper to the teacher, 'Excuse me, do you know whose mum that lady in a striped shirt over there is?'

'Oh, yes. She's Ruru's mom. Ruru Soejima.'

Ruru. Ruru Soejima. I repeat the name in my mind, and a vague memory of her and her family sitting next to us at the entrance ceremony resurfaces. We might have exchanged greetings and briefly introduced ourselves.

'Excuse us, Ms Eri.'

I bow, and I see a badge embroidered with MS ENA sewn on her apron. Oh dear, I got her name wrong.

But the teacher doesn't seem to mind and smiles as she says, 'Goodbye!' before moving on to another mother.

Yes, goodbye. I rush out of the building as if I were fleeing. She must think I'm a foolish parent. Sweat trickles down my forehead, and it's not just because of the heat.

Takumi and I step on to the sidewalk, hand in hand. He looks up at me.

'Mum, do you think Dad got on a plane?'

THE EARNEST ROLLED OMELETTE

'No, he didn't. He took the bullet train to Kyoto.'
'Do bullet trains fly?'
'They don't.'
'Drone beetles can fly.'
'We're not talking about beetles, though.'
'Takumi Express to Kyoto, departing now! All aboard!'

I can't help but burst out laughing as I squeeze his damp hand. The cicadas chirr. That reminds me – a little while ago, Takumi brought home the cast-off shell of a cicada he found with his father. I think about how Teruya and Takumi walk this path together daily, witnessing the changes in the seasons. I suddenly feel left out, and my chest tightens.

My husband, Teruya, spends his time making art. For now, his focus is not on selling his work but simply on painting. We first met at the advertising agency where we both worked. He's two years younger than me, and he was one of my subordinates.

Just before we married, he suddenly declared: 'I want to paint,' before adding, 'If possible, I'd like to quit my job and take care of the household.'

'*What?*' I said, feigning surprise, but deep down, I felt lucky. I'd been living comfortably with my parents until then, never having washed a single rice bowl let alone pressed the switch on a rice cooker.

Work has always been a hundred times more

enjoyable to me than household chores. This would allow me to be the 'breadwinning wife supporting her aspiring artist husband'. It gave me the perfect excuse.

So, I threw myself more intensely into my work while Teruya became a devoted homemaker. He's an exceptional cook, even irons the sheets, and keeps the house spotlessly clean. He also skilfully maintains warm relations with my parents, who live about an hour away by train. During my pregnancy and maternity leave, he took extremely good care of me, and when Takumi was born, he allowed me to sleep in a separate room so I could get proper rest.

Due in part to my challenges with breast milk production, we switched to formula early, and I returned to work sooner than planned. As a result, I don't feel like I've been a proper parent to Takumi. I've never been present for milestone moments like when he stood up or took a step for the first time.

When Takumi started kindergarten, Teruya didn't baulk at the school's requirement for handmade totes and shoe bags. In fact, he seemed delighted, and his sewing was so impeccable that they looked store-bought. 'What if you started selling handmade school accessories to mums who find these kinds of crafts difficult?' I suggested, but he laughed and said, 'I'm not that good.' He has no greed. If Teruya

THE EARNEST ROLLED OMELETTE

had been interested, I would have gladly helped him launch the business. In any event, our family operated with perfect balance. That is, until an invitation arrived from Kyoto.

I knew that Teruya's art, which he shared on Instagram, was being praised for being 'distinct and unique' and that he was gaining followers and comments. But I never imagined it would lead to an invitation to present his work in a group exhibition. A quirky gallery owner in Kyoto was organizing a show featuring works from five emerging painters and illustrators and asked if Teruya might be interested in participating.

Teruya's art is, indeed, intriguing. He makes trick art where multiple images are hidden within a single landscape. Still, I wasn't sure if Teruya and his work stood out among the sea of aspiring artists. At first, I suspected that Teruya might have fallen victim to a scam artist preying on dreamers, so I researched the gallery online. But everything I found checked out. Even with this exhibition, while travel and accommodation aren't covered, there's no 'exhibition fee'. It also seems that events like these have been held several times in the past. The gallery owner is evidently quite well regarded in that world and is known as the 'Maestro' for reasons unknown. He has a plain, smooth face and a prominent mole in the centre of his forehead. Maybe he has influential connections because many artists seem to have taken off with his help.

Receiving a direct message via Instagram from said Maestro, Teruya told me, 'The group exhibition runs Friday to Sunday, but there's the installation and a few meetings, so I want to go to Kyoto directly after dropping Takumi off at kindergarten on Thursday morning. So, could I ask you to take care of picking him up on Thursday as well as drop-off, pick-up, and lunch on Friday? I'll be back on the last train on Sunday.'

I couldn't immediately respond, 'Sure.' The terse response, 'That's impossible. I have work,' was already at the tip of my tongue.

As I remained silent, Teruya said conciliatorily, 'I'll cover travel and lodging expenses myself. I won't use a single yen of the money you've worked hard to make, Asami, so please?'

I was at a loss for words. Has Teruya been living modestly, thinking he had to deprive himself and couldn't use any of the living expenses on himself because he wasn't earning money? Could it be that all this time, he's been dipping into his savings from before we got married to buy his art supplies?

Without thinking, I blurted out, 'That's all right. I'll give you the money, so use it to cover everything,

THE EARNEST ROLLED OMELETTE

OK?' As soon as the words left my mouth, I recognized my error. *I'll give you the money.* I realized how condescending it sounded.

But Teruya didn't seem particularly bothered and said without hesitation, 'No, really, don't worry about it. I've been earning a decent amount myself.'

'What?'

Earning?

As I leaned forward in surprise, Teruya looked down and confessed, 'Yeah, I haven't shared this with you, but my day trading has been going quite well.'

I was speechless. I'd never imagined such a thing. I stared at Teruya, mouth agape.

'Will you be able to watch Takumi?' he asked tentatively.

Well, sure . . . I reluctantly mumbled my assent, but I've been plagued by a nagging anxiety ever since.

Setting all that aside, I must first clear the hurdle right before me. By adjusting my work schedule, I should be able to manage kindergarten drop-off and pick-up. As for meals while Teruya is away, we can eat out or pick up dishes at the department store deli.

The problem is Friday's lunch.

Red, green, black, brown, and then there's yellow – the rolled omelette I can't avoid any longer.

★

After finishing dinner with Takumi at the restaurant and returning home, I stand in the kitchen for my intensive training, frying pan in hand. I've memorized everything I've read on making rolled omelettes in books and on the internet, but for some reason, I can't seem to get it right. They turn out flat instead of fluffy, and the eggs stick to the pan, making it difficult to roll it up neatly. On top of that, different recipes call for different ingredients – some say to add salt, others sugar or soy sauce, and some even potato starch or milk. I can't figure out what we typically do for our version of the rolled omelette, but also I can't bring myself to call Teruya to ask him about it.

Plates of crumbling rolled omelettes are rapidly piling up on the kitchen counter. Takumi, who has been watching TV in the living room, comes over and exclaims, 'Wow!' and innocently asks, 'What's this dish called?'

I feel utterly deflated by his question. I silently crack an egg into a bowl.

An anime theme song begins playing on the TV. Takumi starts dancing and singing along. He hops and whoops out a 'Zoom!' as he makes his way back to the living room, pretending to be a plane.

I beat the eggs with chopsticks. *Swish, swish, swish.* How long do I whisk them for? How long do I cook

THE EARNEST ROLLED OMELETTE

them to get it just right? The vast expanse of yellow before me begins to blur, and I'm surprised to discover I'm crying.

Why? Why can't I even make a rolled omelette?

I studied diligently as a child, and in college I worked hard to land a good job. After I got one, I poured all my energy into my career. I've consistently been recognized for my abilities.

It can't be helped. I've been running away all this time. I've passed off all the chores I hate and the childcare duties I'm not confident about to Teruya, using work as an escape. I've been fleeing from my insecurity about not being able to do the things that everyone else does so effortlessly.

At work, I can tackle anything. I never forget a client's name or face. I'm comfortable voicing my opinions, even to top executives from major corporations. I'm confident in my ability to deliver innovative proposals, present to large audiences and correct my team's errors more effectively than anyone else.

But I don't have a single mum friend, and the circle of mothers at Takumi's kindergarten intimidates me. I can't even remember Takumi's teacher's name. I can't peel an apple without ruining it. I don't know how to sort the trash properly, and folding laundry origami-neat seems like an impossible art form.

The only thing I used to be able to take pride in was that I was financially supporting the household. But I'm not so sure about that any more. I don't know how much Teruya makes from day trading, but I suspect we'll be fine even if we lose my income. What even am I to Teruya and Takumi?

What will I do when Teruya's paintings begin to sell? What should I do if he no longer stays home? I hope his paintings don't sell. I hope no one recognizes his work. I want him to always remain by Takumi's side and mine.

As a silent tear glides down my cheek, my phone rings. I look at the screen. Teruya.

'Answer it – it's your dad.'

I pass my phone to Takumi. He takes the call, bubbling with excitement.

Hi, Dad! Yeah. I ate a hamburger.

I listen absent-mindedly to Takumi's voice, but with the following words, my chopsticks freeze.

'It's awesome. Mum's cooking. It's like a field of flowers – really pretty and yummy-looking!'

I look up with a start. *A field of flowers?* Maybe the green plates gave Takumi that impression. Suddenly, the mound of crumbled eggs seem to be rewarding me with a smile.

'Mum, Dad wants to talk to you,' says Takumi, passing me my phone.

THE EARNEST ROLLED OMELETTE

'Asami? That's incredible! What are you making?'

I'm unable to hold in my sigh when I hear Teruya's kind voice. I move to the back room so Takumi can't hear me and begin weeping. 'Rolled omelettes for lunch. But it's not going well at all. They won't hold their shape, and they're all sticky somehow,' I say, trying to hold in my sobs.

'Are you practising for tomorrow's lunch? You can make scrambled or boiled eggs. You don't have to make a rolled omelette.'

'No, it has to be! In the birthday card Takumi got from kindergarten last year, they wrote that rolled omelette is his favourite food. He's definitely going to be disappointed if there isn't one in his lunch.'

'He's not going to be disappointed.'

'But he *will*! I followed the recipe in the cookbook to the T, but why do I end up with something completely different? Poor Takumi – his useless mother can't even whip up a rolled omelette.'

'*Asami*,' Teruya says sharply. I flinch, thinking he's uncharacteristically angry, but then he asks gently, 'Which frying pan are you using?'

'The red, round one hanging from the wall.'

'That's an old one. The Teflon coating is peeling, which is why the egg's sticking. You probably didn't notice it because it's in a slightly different spot, but we have a rectangular pan specifically for making rolled omelettes. I just replaced it, so it should be easy to use. Can you check under the sink? It has a blue handle.'

I go back into the kitchen, open the cabinet under the sink, and there it is – a small, rectangular frying pan. I remember seeing something like this in the cookbooks. I just assumed they were props used by professional cooks for photo shoots.

'First, heat the pan to scorching, so hot that the eggs will sizzle when you pour them in. A pinch of salt should be enough. Use just a little oil. Don't pour the oil in directly. Dip a folded paper towel in oil and apply it to the pan. I think you might not be waiting long enough before rolling the eggs. I'll stay on the line, so why don't you give it a try?'

I set my phone on the edge of the cabinet and follow Teruya's instructions. The rectangular frying pan is light and easy to handle, and it produces an unbelievably beautiful rolled omelette. By pressing the omelette against the pan's edge, I can shape it further. It isn't perfect, but it's passable.

'It looks like it worked.'

'See?'

Even after I transfer the omelette to a plate, the rectangular pan remains perfectly slick, with no remnants of egg clinging to it.

'What a brilliant frying pan. I couldn't get it right at all with the round one.'

THE EARNEST ROLLED OMELETTE

'The round one's brilliant, too. It's deep and sturdy and the best pan for stir-frying or whipping up mapo tofu. It's also great for boiling small portions of pasta in a pinch. No matter how new and nimble the omelette pan might be, you can't make Chinese food with it. It's all about using the right tools.'

The right tools. I feel reassured by those words. I look admiringly at the large, round frying pan that has worked hard for me. I'm about to thank Teruya when he speaks first.

'You got this. You're an amazing mother, and you're far from useless. Your seriousness and sincerity are what I love about you, Asami.'

The hole that was open inside me slowly fills. I feel Teruya's words have carved out a place for me.

'I hope lots of people come to see your paintings,' I say.

I want to work on household chores little by little. Those words flit across my mind, but I decide to keep them to myself for today. I'll start by wishing Ms Striped Shirt Soejima a good morning first when I see her at the kindergarten tomorrow.

The next thing I know, Takumi is in the kitchen.

'Can I eat this?' he asks.

His silky, round head bobs around my waist. His small hand, pointing at the botched omelettes, resembles a butterfly perched on a flower.

3

Growing Up Together

Pink

'Ms Ena, can I see your hand?' asks Moeka, her big, round eyes looking up at me.

I hesitate. This morning, the instant the mothers departed after drop-off, Moeka bounded up to me eagerly.

'My hands? Here,' I say, spreading my hands wide.

A disappointed expression falls over Moeka's face.

'You don't paint them pink any more?'

'Not any more,' I replied with a smile.

'Why not?'

Because they said I can't. I swallow those words and take Moeka's hand.

'Shall we go over there and read?'

Moeka nods but looks unsatisfied with my response. Her unanswered *Why not?* lingers in the air, coiling around me.

HOT CHOCOLATE ON THURSDAY

It happened last Tuesday.

I'd attended a middle school reunion over the long weekend in September, and, for the first time in a long time, I forgot to remove the polish on my nails after. It's been a year and a half since I started teaching at the kindergarten after graduating from junior college. I might have let my guard down a little.

Technically, there's no regulation forbidding nail polish, but it's more or less an unspoken rule. Some teachers don't even wear make-up.

My nail polish was pink, nothing too flashy, and my nails were trimmed short. I hadn't applied rhinestones or glitter, so there was no risk of anything falling into food or scratching a child. It felt like a safe choice. I decided I would try to get through the day unnoticed. Keeping my hands out of sight as much as possible from the teachers and kindergarteners, I made it through the morning.

It was at lunchtime, while I was distributing cups of milk, when Moeka shouted, 'Wow! Ms Ena, your hands are so pretty.'

I gasped. I wanted to hide them, but I couldn't.

GROWING UP TOGETHER

There were still cups to pass out on my tray. Making sure the other teachers were out of earshot, I whispered, 'Thank you,' then hurriedly set the cup of milk down.

'My mum does it too,' Takumi, the boy with the mushroom haircut seated next to Moeka, declared proudly. 'There's a store that draws on your nails, right?'

In response, Ruru, who was sitting across from them, pounced forward to examine my fingers, nearly dunking the end of her tight braid into her milk. I quickly shifted the cup aside.

'Did you get them done at a store, too, Ms Ena?'

Ruru grabbed my fingers. There was no pretending any more.

'No, I did them myself.'

'You can do it yourself?'

'You can. It's easy.'

I finished passing out the milk, and I fled, wearing a strained smile.

As we were leaving for the day, Moeka approached me. 'Ms Ena, will you please show me your hands again tomorrow?' she whispered.

Moeka looked up at me bashfully, and my gaze dropped to her hands. I swallowed back the gasp of surprise that almost escaped me.

'Tomorrow . . . OK.'

The next day – and the day after that – I went to work without removing my nail polish.

'Will you please come to the office with me?'

It was Friday evening. I was tidying up after school when Ms Yasuko approached me. I could feel my colleagues' worried and inquisitive glances as I followed her.

Ms Yasuko is a veteran teacher of fifteen years. She's one of those who doesn't wear make-up – doesn't even draw her brows. With her well-proportioned features, I think she'd look quite stunning if she wore make-up. She's always been very authoritative, and I've sensed that she never really liked me from the start.

We entered the office. She closed the door behind her, and with no preamble, she commanded, 'Show me your hands.'

I obeyed, and she grabbed my fingers roughly.

'What were you thinking, painting your nails?' she asked. She dropped my hand as if it was something dirty. 'We received a complaint from Ruru Soejima's mother. She's upset because her daughter painted her nails with markers because of you. Apparently, you told the kids that they don't have to go to a salon and that they can paint their own nails. Why would you encourage something like that?'

GROWING UP TOGETHER

Come to think of it, I recalled passing Ruru's mother earlier. When I greeted her, she suddenly turned her face away, and I remember seeing her back in the striped shirt she often wears.

'I didn't encourage—'

'I don't want to hear excuses. The other mothers have noticed, too. It affects not only your reputation but the entire kindergarten's.'

I gritted my teeth. If she'd already decided that I was wrong without listening to my side of the story, there was nothing I could say. As I remained silent, Ms Yasuko kept going.

'Work is work. Personal life is personal life. You must keep them separate, even if you want to doll yourself up for dates with your boyfriend after work or whatever.'

No, that isn't true at all! I was about to refute her, but I stopped myself. Ms Yasuko always thinks she's right. It was pointless to try to explain myself. In my own way, I was doing my best at work. Besides, I didn't know how to justify keeping my nail polish on, nor did I feel confident that my reasoning was correct.

'Anyway, remove your nail polish, OK?'

'I will,' I finally squeezed out. I clenched my fists tightly as if to hide my pink nails.

That night, as I soaked a cotton ball in nail-polish

remover, I found myself reminiscing about my cousin Maco. I idolized Maco when I was little. Many years older than me, she was pretty and intelligent. She'd taught me everything from how to tie my hair, wrap my scarf and paint my nails.

Maco, who had studied abroad in Sydney, Australia in high school, graduated from college with a degree in education. She now works as an English teacher at a language school. She once told me why she chose to work at a language school instead of becoming a traditional school teacher: 'I want to be around people willing to spend money to study English again so they can speak it properly. I want to be around enthusiastic people actively trying to grasp something on their own, rather than just completing assigned lessons to score well on tests.'

Maco had a massive influence on my decision to study education at junior college. I liked the idea of being a teacher, but that was about the only thing we had in common. I felt like I'd chosen this path without any true sense of purpose or reason. I thought, *Kids are cute*. That was about it.

Once I'd removed all my nail polish, I lay on my bed and took out my phone. I went to the *CANVAS* website that I'd bookmarked. *CANVAS* is a free newspaper published in Sydney for the Japanese community and features restaurant guides, event information and local job listings. While Maco was studying abroad, she was interviewed for a story and became friendly with the editor, and through that connection, she still contributes to the paper. While the physical paper is available only in Sydney, the online articles can be read from Japan, so I often check them out.

I was aimlessly browsing various sections, my unvarnished nails gliding up and down the screen. But I abruptly stopped scrolling when I came across an article titled 'Working Holiday Experiences'.

I'd heard about working holidays before. It's a visa that allows you to travel, study and work abroad for a year. Didn't a senior colleague in her late twenties resign to go on a 'last-minute' working holiday? By 'last-minute', I believe she was referring to going before reaching the programme's age limit of thirty. I should still have a chance.

I typed the terms 'Australia' and 'working holiday' into a search engine and eagerly read all the results that popped up.

To be eligible to apply for a working holiday, you have to be between the ages of eighteen and thirty, have about four hundred and fifty thousand yen for living expenses and be in good health. You can complete the application online as long as you have a passport, credit card and an application fee of just under forty thousand yen. There is no exam and no need to even visit the Australian embassy. Huh, it turned out it's pretty easy to go on a working holiday.

On these sites, there were countless photos of Japanese travellers with their arms around the shoulders of Australians, diving into the ocean, shearing sheep. Australia seemed very safe and full of Japanophiles. I once thought that only people fluent in English and independent, like Maco, could live abroad, but I was learning that it might be less challenging than I initially thought.

It sounds like a good idea . . .?

Didn't it sound much better than my current life – a low-paying job, bullying colleagues, complaining mothers, and not even the freedom to paint my nails? I could do something else in Australia. I wasn't sure what exactly yet, but I'd think of something. There were things I could do there that I couldn't do here. I was young, healthy and outgoing. I might even find an Australian boyfriend. I could figure out my reason for going to Australia once I was there. If I returned to Japan fluent in English, I could work for a foreign company. Or become an interpreter or even something like a purchasing buyer – that would be cool. I should be able to accomplish that if I start working on it now, right?

Should I quit the kindergarten?
Should I leave?

It's mid-October when I learn from the principal that Moeka is leaving our kindergarten. She's moving the next week because of her father's sudden job transfer.

At pick-up time, Moeka's mother calls out to me.

'Ms Ena! Thank you for taking good care of my daughter.'

She is usually quiet and reserved; this is the first time she has initiated a conversation with me.

'I heard you're moving.'

'Yes.' There's a pause.

Just when I feel compelled to fill the silence, Moeka's mother speaks up again.

'Moeka has stopped biting her nails,' she says with a quiet smile. 'She used to chew on all her fingernails, and sometimes, it was so bad they would bleed. I was really concerned. The parenting books said you shouldn't scold and that it's caused by a lack of affection . . . I felt like I was giving her all my love. Yet, I couldn't help feeling I was at fault.'

I don't know quite how to respond.

'About a month ago, Moeka was so excited to tell me how pretty and pink your nails were and that she wanted her hands to look just as pretty. That's when she decided, on her own, that she wouldn't bite her nails any more. Her nails used to be all jagged and never got the chance to grow, but now they're nice and even,' says Moeka's mother, her voice quivering.

I feel my own heart swell and my eyes brim with tears. *Oh, what a relief.* My quiet hope paid off. Just as I had once admired Maco, I thought that if Moeka found my pink nails lovely, she might stop biting her own.

Moeka's mother bows deeply. 'Thank you very much.'

'B-but I removed my nail polish almost right away, so I worried Moeka might have been disappointed,' I say, stumbling over my words.

'Not at all,' says Moeka's mum, straightening. 'In fact, she thought your nails were beautiful after you removed the polish.'

'What?'

'Haven't you heard from Ms Yasuko?'

I have heard nothing. The mere mention of Ms Yasuko is unexpected.

'At first, Moeka thought your painted nails were cute – that was the initial draw. But after you removed the polish, Ms Yasuko told the class that your hands were those of a hard worker. That they would have beautiful nails like yours if they laughed a lot, ate well and tackled everything with joy. That once they grew up, if they decided to be stylish and paint their nails, it'd look stunning on healthy ones.'

Ms Yasuko said that? I am stunned.

Moeka's mother looks at her own hand.

'Nails are indicators of health, aren't they? I've neglected mine recently. My husband's been so busy with work and hasn't been home much, and I feel like I've been carrying the burden of parenting alone. It's been wearing me down. With this move, I think we'll be able to spend more time together as a family. I want to stay happy and healthy so Moeka and I can have beautiful pink nails someday.'

When Moeka's mother smiles, her eyes look just like her daughter's.

We hear Moeka's cheerful voice call out, 'Mum!' and I see her come running.

'It's sad, isn't it, saying goodbye?'

I spin around, nearly leaping out of my skin, and come face to face with Ms Yasuko. Seeing my reaction – as if I've spotted a snake – Ms Yasuko frowns.

'You don't have to be so surprised. I've been standing here, waiting to say goodbye, but it didn't seem like the right moment for me to step in.'

Ms Yasuko averts her gaze and observes Moeka and her mother walk towards the gate.

I start to say, 'Umm—' but Ms Yasuko cuts me off.

'I wasn't defending you exactly. But, well . . .' She finally looks me in the eye. 'You do work hard.'

I'm bewildered by Ms Yasuko's unusually gentle tone. Maybe she understands me better than I think. The thought makes me a little emotional.

Spotting my reaction, Ms Yasuko's tone hardens. 'If you'd explained yourself properly, I wouldn't have reprimanded you so harshly. You should've just talked to me about it instead of sulking in silence.'

Her usual sternness doesn't intimidate me this time. It's not because Ms Yasuko has changed, but rather, my perspective, my way of receiving her words, has shifted.

'I didn't know how to explain myself. I also understand why Ruru's mother was angry with me,' I reply.

Ms Yasuko's expression turns serious.

'Even if you're unsure, I want you to talk to me. I've been there. When I was around your age, I used to wear tinted lip balm – it wasn't quite lipstick – but, once, when I was carrying a boy, it got on his shirt. His mother accused me of being improper.'

'That's awful . . .'

'No, I was wrong. That's why I've avoided wearing anything with colour. On the other hand, some mothers say wearing a little make-up is proper grooming for adults. Everyone has their own opinion. Even with your nails, I think it's undeniable they helped Moeka kick her nail-biting habit. But it won't always turn out well, and not all parents will approve. What's best for the children is something we must judge on a case-by-case basis.'

I nod. I feel strangely calm.

Every moment is like a live performance. Through trial and error and taking things head-on, we continue to search for answers we don't even know are right. You could almost see the children growing up every day. As I face each one, I'm sure that I, too, am growing.

'It's difficult. It's challenging . . . but I've come to understand that's what makes this work so rewarding,' I say.

'Oh, how cheeky,' teases Ms Yasuko. 'I've always been concerned about you, and perhaps I've been a bit tough on you. You know, you remind me of my younger self.'

'*What?*' I recoil reflexively.

'Why does that bother you?!'

'I'm not bothered!'

We laugh together. It's a first, but I feel like I've been waiting for a long time to talk with Ms Yasuko like this.

Ahh, I've found it, I thought.

I won't quit my job today. For now, I'm going to keep trying my best here. Because it brings me so much happiness that Moeka wants to have beautiful nails, that Moeka's mother smiled so peacefully, and that I have a connection with Ms Yasuko. There is still so much I want to do at this kindergarten. That's my reason for being here.

Ms Yasuko and I watch the parents and children leave. *See you tomorrow. Stay happy and well.* At the gate, Moeka turns around and waves enthusiastically at us.

4

A Saint's Righteous Path

Blue

Risa traces the rim of her teacup with a finger and asks, 'Do you know that "something old" rhyme?'

We used to go on what we called 'gourmet tours', eating our way around different restaurants, but with her wedding coming up next month, she's on a diet. Apparently, December is off-season for weddings, which means lower costs.

It's been a while since we last saw each other, yet she didn't ask to go for a drink or lunch but suggested we meet for tea in the early afternoon. The Marble Cafe, where Risa has brought me, is on the other side of the river from the kindergarten where I work. It's hidden behind the row of cherry blossom trees, and I hadn't been aware of its existence until now. It's bright and well maintained. On the wall, there's a piece of trick art painted by an artist who's been the talk of the town lately. The young waiter works briskly and occasionally casts a gentle, watchful glance our way.

I take a sip of my café au lait and answer Risa. 'Yes, I know it. It's part of an English wedding rhyme, right?'

'Is it?' Risa looks surprised even though she's the one who brought it up.

Something old, something new, something borrowed, something blue. The things, according to an old English saying, that will bring good luck to a bride if she wears them on her wedding day. The rhyme also mentions *A silver sixpence in her shoe*, but that line is often left out.

'You would know your rhymes – a true kindergarten teacher! A gold star for Ms Yasuko!' teases Risa, but I just look out of the window without saying a word.

We've been close friends since high school. We can talk about anything. We shared many experiences, including our boyfriend-less histories.

One Christmas, when we were both thirty, Risa said, 'If we're both single when we turn sixty, let's live together.' I laughed and replied, '*Ugh*, I hope we're not, but I guess we might have to.' Of course, we both wanted to find partners. It was just a little joke single girls often make and nothing serious enough to be called a promise. Six years have passed since then.

A SAINT'S RIGHTEOUS PATH

Two years ago, at an Italian trattoria, Risa told me she was seeing someone – someone she hoped to marry. I thought to myself, *Shit*. That was when we were thirty-four, right in the thick of the second wave of the wedding rush.

I remember back in high school, the two of us dreaded the school marathon. Risa promised we'd stick together during the race, but when we got to the final stretch, I remember her pulling ahead of me. Well, I didn't really care. The marathon wasn't all that important to me. I just recall thinking to myself, *This is so typical of her.*

The moment the word 'marriage' came out of Risa's mouth, the memory of her back fading into the distance at that marathon flitted through my mind, but I managed to force out a 'Congratulations'. After all, it was good news. It'd be a shame for us both if I didn't smile at this moment.

But when she lowered her head and said, 'He's in the middle of divorce mediation,' my fake smile instantly crumbled. 'He's been separated from his wife since before we met—'

'No way, don't go through with it,' I said, interrupting her explanation. 'Not with a guy like that. He's just saying that. He's not going to get divorced. You're almost in your mid-thirties – what are you doing?'

As I ranted, Risa quietly said, 'You wouldn't understand.'

I was speechless. I thought I understood everything about Risa. And she about me.

The clinking of fork against plate resonated from the next table over. As I kept my gaze averted, Risa said, 'You're really lucky. You have skills and a job that you love. Teaching kindergarten – it's a profession that earns respect, and the longer you work in it, the more trust you build. I'm just a temp office worker. I don't have any particular skills or qualifications. I spend my days worrying about when I might be let go.'

I've had many people say things like this to me. *It's great that you have a skill you can rely on. You'll never be out of work. Must be nice to be paid to play with children.* Give me a break! If you think all I do at the kindergarten is sing, play the piano and frolic with the kids and that my day is over when the children go home, you're entirely mistaken. It's hard for people to believe, but I sometimes have to bring work home and stay up all night to finish it. And even when new staff join, the young ones quit right away. On top of that, we have to deal with the parents' complaints and demanding requests, which is much worse than handling the kids.

Until now, the only person to whom I could vent about these things was Risa. So, I was utterly taken

A SAINT'S RIGHTEOUS PATH

aback when she made those remarks. Especially since the temp job she complained about came through her uncle's connection. I studied hard, searched for a job and landed this position all on my own. I don't want to be told I'm 'lucky' so casually.

I lashed out at Risa. 'Qualifications are just a matter of whether you choose to get them or not. You can still study and pick up new skills. Using marriage as an escape is just naive.'

'It's not like that . . . I feel—'

'If he's in the middle of divorce mediation, doesn't that mean he's still legally married? So, isn't what you guys have considered an affair? Are you sure you're not being led on with the promise of marriage?'

Risa stayed silent for a moment.

'I knew you wouldn't understand.'

'I guess not.' I said nothing more.

I didn't understand, and I didn't want to understand. That's what I believed. Risa didn't understand me either. I, too, had my struggles.

After that, things became too awkward, and we stopped contacting each other.

About a year after our falling out at the trattoria, I received a New Year's card from Risa that stated, 'His divorce has been finalized.' My honest reaction was one of disbelief. I had been sure things wouldn't work out, and having more or less told her that back then, I couldn't bring myself to reach out, so I left things as they were. Besides, congratulating her on the divorce felt inappropriate, even though I was curious about the details.

Then, in October, Risa called me to tell me that she was getting married and we somewhat made amends. When a wedding invitation arrived, I confirmed my attendance.

And here we are today, meeting over tea. Through the spotlessly polished window of the cafe, I can see the autumn leaves fluttering down gracefully.

'Of the four "somethings", I think I have three. For the old item, my mother's pearl necklace; the new, a lace handkerchief; something borrowed, the opera gloves my sister wore at her wedding. I haven't decided on the something blue.'

Something blue. It's true that it's hard to picture something blue with an entirely white wedding dress. *You should just carry your wedding blues in your heart*, I think, but I quickly admonish myself for having such mean thoughts. Oblivious to my inner ugliness, Risa leans in. 'I heard it's best to wear it where it can't be seen. Apparently, it's common in some countries to wear a blue ribbon on your garter.'

'Garter?'

'Yup. But I've actually never seen garters in real life.' Risa turns crimson.

A SAINT'S RIGHTEOUS PATH

There is nothing lewd about garters, but this sort of innocence is so characteristic of Risa.

'Why not give it a try? Your first garter,' I say with a laugh.

Risa frantically waves off the suggestion.

'*No way*. I don't even like the colour blue to begin with. It feels kind of cold to me.'

'Really? I like blue. I get a virtuous and sincere vibe from it.'

'You would feel that.' Risa sighs softly.

There's an awkward silence. I startle when I realize that we must both be thinking about our fight. For a while, we remain quiet, avoiding eye contact. I down my café au lait and even finish my glass of water.

It's Risa who breaks the silence. After taking a long sip of her tea, she says, 'Remember when I said, "I knew you wouldn't understand"?'

'Yeah.'

'I'm sorry I said something so pathetic then. It's been bothering me ever since.'

'It's fine.'

'I've always, always admired you. Since high school, you've known what you've wanted to do and walked straight down your chosen path. As for me, I kept getting lost, taking detours and side paths . . . I didn't have it – something that made my heart burn with passion. I'm not very smart, so it's hard to put this in words, but I think we don't get to choose to be passionate. Wanting to do this, wanting to have that, or wanting to be a certain way – to desire something – it's all up to the universe's will.'

I'm stunned. This is the first time I've seen Risa speak so assertively. A man reading the sports section of a newspaper at the counter glances over at us. Risa is so riled up that I hesitate to caution her to lower her voice.

'But when I met him for the first time, I thought, *I really, really want to be with him*. Maybe it's immoral, but I just wanted to marry him. No one else would do.'

Risa's eyes shine brightly as if taken over by the so-called universe's will. I don't quite get it. Isn't 'desire' simply wanting what I want?

'But you know, desire is amazing, isn't it? Desire begets more desire. All I wished for was to be his wife, and now that it's about to come true, I . . .' She hesitates for a moment, then says quietly but clearly, 'I want to be a mother.' She shrugs. 'I didn't know I could be so greedy. It scares me a little.'

I'm fumbling for the right words when a phone buzzes. Risa reaches into her bag.

'It's Hiroyuki. Excuse me for a moment.'

Risa steps outside the cafe with just her phone.

A SAINT'S RIGHTEOUS PATH

Left on my own, I feel a little befuddled. Is Hiroyuki her fiancé?

Risa has always been this way. She acts all troubled, but everything always works out for her. We're complete opposites. How did we end up best friends? Were we even best friends in the first place? What connected us? Why were we together all the time? What was it about Risa that I liked so much? I would never leave my friend alone at a moment like this to answer a call.

'Take your own sweet time, why don't you?' I mutter.

'I-I'm so sorry,' a voice stammers from behind.

I spin around and see the server with a pitcher in his hand. It seems he was just about to refill my water glass.

'Oh, no. I wasn't addressing you just now.'

The server bows and pours water into my glass. His smiling face is fresh and clean, as if he's just stepped out of the bath. He's young, probably around the same age as Ms Ena, who has been working with me for two years. There's a dignified air and a sense of old-fashioned politeness about him.

'I'm annoyed that my friend, who was sitting here, left in the middle of our conversation to take a call,' I explain.

The server tilts back his pitcher and smiles.

'From my point of view, her stepping outside shows courtesy and consideration to the other customers.'

I'm taken aback. What I consider unreasonable might seem sensible from a different perspective.

'I've always tried to choose the straightest path, and I've expected the same from others ... but maybe I'm mistaken,' I say.

'Hmm ... I think what matters isn't whether the path is straight or not but doing your best to walk as straight as possible, even on a winding path.'

Those words suddenly bring back a memory from that school marathon. It was around a bend close to the finish line when Risa started sprinting at full speed. Our maths teacher stood on the sidelines. He was a superficial and unbelievably tyrannical man who did nothing but look down on his students. One time, when Risa and I were hanging out during a break, he walked by us and said to Risa, 'Don't you go infecting Yasuko with your stupidity. Stay away from her.'

At the time, Risa laughed weakly, but looking back, I realize she began to keep her distance from me whenever he was around. Maybe because I'd already dismissed him as a brainless jerk, I hadn't taken his words very seriously. But Risa must have felt their sting. That's why she ran so hard to get away from me during the race. I was a fool not to realize something so obvious.

A SAINT'S RIGHTEOUS PATH

'It's not easy to put yourself in someone else's shoes...'

'That's true. But even if you get it wrong, the fact that you're thinking of the other person might still come across. And sometimes, just imagining what the other person is thinking can be fun,' says the server. He grins as if remembering something.

He's a sincere, straightforward kid. I smile and take a swig of my water.

'I hope things work out with the person whose thoughts you're imagining,' I say.

In an instant, crimson spreads across the server's face.

Risa returns.

'I'm sorry. Hiroyuki's grandmother fell this morning and injured herself. She thought she might have broken a bone, but after being checked at the hospital, it seems like it's just a bruise and should heal with two days of rest. His grandmother lives alone, so we were worried... I'm glad she's OK.'

Ahh, it was a call she couldn't miss.

'Shouldn't you have gone with her to the hospital?'

'Hiroyuki told me to not to worry about it since I had plans to see an important friend. And I also really wanted to see you today.'

The way she speaks her mind so candidly and sincerely like this dazzles me.

Ever since I was in school, people have disliked me. Maybe 'disliked' is too strong – 'avoided' and 'feared' might be more accurate. Even so, I was constantly being pushed into the role of class representative. No one ever volunteered for those positions, so the teacher would appoint me. I performed my duties diligently, but that only made me even less popular. I couldn't see what was wrong with calling out boys who shirked cleaning duties or girls who talked during class.

In my limited dating experience, the guys who left always said things like, 'I feel suffocated around you' or 'I don't like to be forced to accept your "correct" opinions'.

Risa was the only one who was different.

She was slow, timid and a crybaby. Yet, for some reason, she didn't avoid or fear me – she opened her heart to me with no hesitation. *I feel safe around you, Yasuko. I can talk to you about anything because you never talk behind someone's back or tell a lie just to get by.*

It was similar to how children seem drawn to me. Even kids who look stone-faced at adults who coo 'Aren't you adorable!' at them will gravitate towards me. That's what made me want to work with children. I wanted to teach them what I consider the straight path. I was tired of being among adults who treated integrity as if it were a flaw.

A SAINT'S RIGHTEOUS PATH

'Risa, I'm sorry, but can you wait here for fifteen, no, ten minutes?'

I dash out of the Marble Cafe. I recall seeing a sign for a lingerie store in a building across the bridge, near the station. I run as fast as I can.

If it were me, I wouldn't have fallen in love with a married man.

If it were me, I wouldn't be embarrassed to wear a garter.

If it were me, I wouldn't prepare any of the 'somethings' for my wedding.

But.

If it were Risa.

I get to the store and go down to the basement. There's a single curly-haired shop assistant in the dimly lit store. I'm looking not for garters but for panties. It seems there's only one of each item in this store.

Navy, aqua – pretty, but not what I'm looking for. I finally find something in the perfect shade of blue. But it's in a polka dot print and is too lacy . . . no, that's not what I'm looking for.

I spot a pair of glossy, satiny panties inside the display case by the cash register.

'Excuse me, can you show me these?'

The shop assistant takes out the undergarment from the case.

'They're silk and feel great on the skin.'

The design is simple, elegant and a refreshing royal blue. This is it.

'Wonderful. I'd like to gift this to a dear friend. Could you wrap it up?'

As the shop assistant wraps it as gently as one might a delicate cake, she says, 'I'm glad you picked this one. I'm most proud of this piece.'

After she finishes wrapping it, she places it in a paper bag with the store's logo and hands it to me. 'Here you go. The style name of the panties is "Maria".'

My breath catches.

'Maria?'

'Yes. Blue is the colour of the Virgin Mary. Just as Mother Teresa's habit had a blue border that symbolized the same.'

It all seems a bit too perfect. I can't help but smile as I accept the package.

The Virgin Mary is the mother of all mothers. *Blue isn't a cold colour at all, Risa.*

I rush back to the Marble Cafe and find Risa absent-mindedly gazing out of the window.

Out of breath, I slide into the seat across from her.

'Here. A "something blue" that'll stay hidden. Panties. Even if you're too embarrassed to wear a wedding garter, you'll wear underwear, right? Let me give them to you as a gift.'

A SAINT'S RIGHTEOUS PATH

'Wait. Did you go buy underwear just now?'

'I did. Any problem with that?'

Oh, *why* do I always end up sounding so arrogant? I was just feeling awkward. But Risa is giggling. Her laughter has always been my salvation.

'Hmm, how uncharacteristic of you to do something so spontaneous.'

Even though I told her what I'd got her, Risa begins opening the package right there and then.

When she sees the panties, she lets out a 'Wow' and pulls them out on to the table.

'So pretty . . . thank you. Now I've got everything.'

This isn't the right place to spread out lingerie, I think to myself, but seeing Risa's joyous smile makes me so happy that I say this instead: 'Children can be challenging.'

Risa looks up at me, the panties still in her hand.

I continue, 'They're challenging and adorable and funny and vulnerable and strong. You can't take your hands or eyes off of them. Just when you think you've figured them out, they've grown up on their own. They understand things far better than you can imagine. Truly, they're monsters.'

Risa is listening intently, and I look her straight in the eye.

'So, if you want a child, be prepared. There's nothing wrong with being greedy. What's wrong with wanting to be a mother? Be an extremely greedy woman, love Hiroyuki with all your heart and welcome the baby that'll one day grow right there in your belly.'

Risa is looking down, my gift clutched tightly in her hands. Her lips are downturned, and her eyes are wide open – she looks somewhat angry. I'm very familiar with that expression. It's the one she wears when holding back tears.

'Risa,' I say, and she lifts her face. 'Congratulations.'

When I finally manage to say those words, Risa's face crumples, and her tears begin to flow.

A week after the wedding, I receive a postcard from their honeymoon in Sydney.

'We've been blessed with great weather, and we've been having a wonderful time. The sky is truly as gorgeous as it is on this postcard!'

Endless azure stretches across the postcard. I pin the beautiful blue securely to the wall so it never falls out of place.

5

A Chance Encounter

Red

If we get separated, let's meet in front of the giraffes – that's what we agreed before heading in together. But I lost sight of Hiroyuki almost instantly, and I've now been staring at the giraffes for fifteen minutes.

Taronga Zoo is one of Australia's largest zoos. I can barely visualize what twenty-one hectares look like, but it's so vast that I can't even muster the energy to search for him. The guidebook said there are over three hundred and forty species of animals here. The giraffe enclosure is the fourth from the entrance. It'll take a whole day just to make a lap around the premises, and if I'm stuck waiting like this, I won't get to see any of the other animals. The koalas were sleeping, and I haven't even seen the kangaroos and emus yet.

December is the height of summer in Sydney, and though it's dry and not as humid as Tokyo, the sun is incredibly strong. I am wearing my hat low over my eyes as I sip from a bottle of sparkling water.

Taronga Zoo is located right by the sea. This morning, we took a ferry from the Circular Quay to get here. Beyond the giraffe enclosure, you can see Sydney Harbour and, beyond that, a dense cluster of high-rise buildings. Giraffes, the sea and skyscrapers – it's a truly peculiar view.

Last night, I picked up a copy of a Japanese-language free newspaper at a Japanese restaurant in town. The publication, called *CANVAS*, seems to be tailored more for Japanese expats in Sydney rather than tourists. Finding a spot shaded from direct sunlight, I unfold my copy of *CANVAS*.

I find a feature on Christmas. 'Does Australia's Santa Claus Arrive on a Surfboard?' Come to think of it, that's next week already. There's an illustration of a Santa Claus in sunglasses and a red swimsuit riding a surfboard. *Right, it's the middle of summer.* I find myself chuckling at this rather flashy Santa.

But it must be hard. On a sleigh, the reindeer carry Santa and his presents, but surfing requires athleticism. He'll have to be careful not to get the gifts wet, and crossing the ocean alone must be lonely. If I were Santa Claus and I were deployed to Australia, I definitely couldn't do it. I've never even surfed before. As I think about this, I scan the place for Hiroyuki.

A CHANCE ENCOUNTER

Hiroyuki is a good person. He was the section manager at the third company I was placed at through the temp agency. He's gentle, generous and doesn't mind doing chores. When I make mistakes, he never says anything snide. He never speaks arrogantly to waitstaff at restaurants, which I really appreciate. When we were planning our honeymoon, I said, 'Sydney would be nice,' to which he responded, 'Sounds good. Let me look into it.' Not 'Whatever you want' or 'Not Sydney'. And he did really 'look into it' and found several travel agencies and tour packages. He's very thoughtful.

We registered our marriage on the morning of our wedding, and immediately after the ceremony, we boarded a plane. It's our second day in Sydney, so I've only been Hiroyuki's wife for three days. *Wife.* I'm Hiroyuki's wife. The thought fills me with a deep sense of relief and an equally deep sense of gnawing anxiety.

I fold the paper and stow it in my bag. I glance at my watch. Twenty minutes have passed. Hiroyuki still hasn't come.

One of the giraffes vigorously bends its neck. A neck that long must be inconvenient. When giraffes catch colds and have sore throats, I wonder where exactly they feel the pain. Every time they blink, their eyelashes, thick like lash extensions, seem to rustle.

For a while now, a pair of giraffes have been standing near me, not engaging in conversation (of course) or looking at each other. They munch on leaves and stare at the buildings in the distance.

'Oh, how chic,' I hear a voice say behind me. When I turn around, I see a petite elderly woman standing beside an elderly man of similar stature.

Of course, she's not referring to me, but rather, the giraffe.

'The pattern of its coat is beautiful, but its tail also has flair.'

'It also looks like it's wearing a crown.'

They are chatting to each other warmly. If I remember correctly, I saw this couple in the lobby at Narita International Airport. Their suitcase had the same luggage tag that the travel agency had given us, so I remember thinking they must have signed up for the same tour. What a happy-looking couple. Perhaps noticing me gazing at them, the lady smiles at me.

'Hello. We were on the same flight, weren't we?'

'Yes, we were.'

'Where's your travel companion?'

'Well, actually, we got separated.'

I look down, feeling embarrassed.

'Is that so? Are you newlyweds?'

'We've only been married for three days.'

A CHANCE ENCOUNTER

Oh my! The elderly man and woman exclaim in unison and laugh. It isn't only their physiques that are similar; their faces also look alike. They are like two peas nestled happily in a pod.

'In such a large zoo, it'll be really hard to find each other.'

'It's OK. We agreed to meet in front of the giraffes if we got separated. If I wait here, he'll eventually show up. It happens quite often, his suddenly wandering off.' I let out a self-deprecating laugh.

That's exactly right. Hiroyuki is a good person, but sometimes, he's hard to figure out. He's a little too free-spirited, and it perplexes me. He's normally very kind, but I feel blindsided when he casually leaves me on my own. It makes my anxiety bubble up: maybe he doesn't care for me as much as I thought.

And, while I try not to dwell on it, another source of worry is the fact that he's a divorcé. He was already separated from his wife when I met him, so I've been telling myself that I didn't steal him from her.

When I first met him, I absolutely knew I wanted to marry him. It was the first time I'd felt such passion. Only after my wish finally came true did I start wondering why things hadn't worked out with his previous wife. I don't think it's right for me to ask him about it, and part of me doesn't even want to know. In a sense, it's none of my business.

But even with his previous wife, they must have loved each other to get married. They must have exchanged vows of eternal love at their wedding. Why do so many couples end up divorced when they're supposed to have been bound by the red thread of fate? There's no guarantee that the same won't happen to us.

Several elementary-school-age boys, letting out whoops, come running. Likely local kids, they scream English words I don't understand as they dart away. Even with all their shouting, the noise doesn't bother me, maybe because the grounds are so vast. The paths are neatly paved, but the animals appear to be enjoying themselves in nature, surrounded by trees and flowers. It feels like I'm in a small jungle.

'Even when he wanders off, he comes back every time, right?' asks the lady.

I look up at her. 'That's true, but it feels disheartening to come all the way to Sydney and have this happen.'

'I understand. But when you come to a place like this, it's so fun and unusual, you can't help but let your curiosity take over and run off in all directions.' The lady giggles.

Her gentle eyes ease my heart.

'How long have you two been married?'

A CHANCE ENCOUNTER

'Fifty years. We're here to celebrate our anniversary. Our only daughter gifted this trip to us. It must have been two years ago when Peep – Peep is what we call our daughter – attended her childhood friend's wedding in Sydney. She told us what a lovely city it was.'

A grin spreads across the woman's face, and the corners of the man's lips lift at almost exactly the same angle. When I say, 'What a good daughter you have!' the lady becomes even more garrulous.

'She runs a lingerie store in Tokyo. She's always been very crafty and loves needlework. She used to sew dresses and such, but she became passionate about undergarments. Now she designs and sells one-of-a-kind pieces – bras, panties, that kind of thing. If you're interested, you should check out her store next time.'

'Sure,' I say, and nod. It's astonishing to think that a whole human being emerged from this little old lady. A baby who learned to walk. A little girl who grew up into an adult who gifted her parents a trip and now runs her own store. If these two hadn't come together, she would never have existed.

How amazing. The birth of a person into this world is truly amazing.

When I told my best friend Yasuko, a kindergarten teacher, that I wanted a child, she said something like, 'If you want a child, be prepared.' Before I met Hiroyuki, I'd never once thought I wanted to be a mother. I always believed myself incapable of giving birth and raising a child. But once I decided to marry Hiroyuki, I thought for the first time: I'd like to meet his child.

Until now, I've never longed for anything. Feelings of 'love' or 'desire' were things that spontaneously appeared from somewhere far away. It's a kind of talent, really. I wasn't blessed with much talent. So when I fell so deeply in love with Hiroyuki, a married man, and found myself wanting a child, I surprised even myself. My only explanation for this longing is that Hiroyuki is my soulmate. But I also carry an unspeakable worry: what if he isn't my soulmate after all?

'Your destinies must be connected by the red thread of fate if you've got along for the past fifty years,' I say, full of admiration.

The old lady's expression turns serious. 'Red thread?!'

'Of fate?!' chimes in the old man.

They exchange looks and burst into laughter.

' "Red thread of fate"! I didn't know there are still romantic young ladies who believe in that!' says the man. His tone isn't mocking but instead filled with admiration.

A CHANCE ENCOUNTER

The old lady waves her hand before her face. 'We didn't always get along, not all fifty years. We've been through our fair share of ups and downs. It's more like, somehow, fifty years have gone by, and here we are.'

'Have you ever wanted to get a divorce?'

'Oh, definitely. Many times. And who knows what the future holds!'

Really? Is this how things are supposed to be?

'Is eternal love difficult to achieve?'

I expect them to exclaim 'Eternal love!' again, but the two don't laugh this time.

'Hmm. It's both difficult and easy to achieve. You can't just decide to love something. Love is a free and mercurial thing.'

The lady looks up at the giraffes. The slightly larger giraffe leans its neck closer to the smaller one.

'Maybe that's why people go out of the way to vow eternal love at their weddings.'

Animals don't go out of the way to pledge anything. The two giraffes lightly touch necks and begin grooming each other's manes.

'Risa.'

I hear someone call my name, and I turn towards the voice. Hiroyuki is standing behind me, having appeared without my noticing.

'I'm sorry. I was so captivated I got carried away. I

saw a platypus over there. They say it doesn't often come out around people, but I was lucky and got there just as it was going for a swim. Let's go check it out together.'

Hiroyuki is pink-cheeked and bouncing with joy. I was so lonely being left behind, but when I see Hiroyuki so happy, I can't help but forgive him.

The lady smiles at Hiroyuki.

'Hello, husband of three days.'

'Hello,' says Hiroyuki, seemingly unsurprised by the sudden greeting. I admire how he's always unfazed.

'They were keeping me company while I was waiting for you,' I say.

'Oh, thank you very much,' he says, bowing to them. He looks at the couple and says cheerfully, 'You look just like each other, as if you were twins!'

I tense up, alarmed by Hiroyuki's impolite comment to people he's just met. But the old man bursts into raucous laughter and says, 'We're often told that.'

Hiroyuki asks, 'Did you grow to resemble each other, or did you look like each other from the start?'

'Hmm, I wonder,' the man replies. 'I'd say rather than growing to resemble each other, we're becoming the same.'

'Oh, so, like, you share the same hobbies and tastes in food?'

A CHANCE ENCOUNTER

'Not quite . . . More like the other becomes me, and I become the other.'

It feels like he's said something profound, and I swallow hard.

Hiroyuki, too, seems very intrigued and says, 'That's philosophical.'

'Well, it's something to look forward to in fifty years,' says the man, chuckling.

'When you say "become the other", do you mean you become one in body and soul?' I ask.

The lady places a hand on her cheek. 'That sounds tiring. How should I say this? Somehow – and I know this might sound odd – at some point, it started to surprise me that we're not related by blood.'

When Hiroyuki says, 'You *do* look alike,' the lady shakes her head from side to side.

'No, no. Our appearance has nothing to do with it. Sometimes, I find it hard to believe we're not blood relations. You know how in a family tree, there's first-degree relatives, second-degree relatives, and such? It surprises me that he and I are not relatives *at all*. I just can't believe it; I feel a deeper connection with this person than with anyone else on Earth. It feels like my body's confused.'

'Oh, wow, that's amazing. To think that you could even confuse your genes,' says Hiroyuki, laughing loudly. I, on the other hand, am too moved to laugh.

Red threads of fate are not merely flimsy lines that connect one pinkie finger to another but perhaps the blood that courses through each other's bodies. It's not about reeling in threads that have been connected beforehand. It's about resonating with the myriad threads flowing within us through our various experiences. Maybe we're all continually searching for a special connection like that.

I look up at Hiroyuki's kind profile. I don't know what the next fifty years will hold, but in this moment, I want to be with him for all of them. I have someone I feel this way about, smiling next to me – there's nothing more precious. Undoubtedly, it's moments like this that will shape us.

Hiroyuki catches my eye and grins. I can feel our blood coursing. It's OK. I have the 'talent' to love. This is fine, I nod silently. I am happy.

Even if it's not fated. Or eternal. Or pledged.

6

A Half-Century Romance

Silver

Good morning. What beautiful weather again today. Have you eaten already?

I don't feel entirely at ease having breakfast at the hotel's open-air cafe, but it's nice to be fancy every now and then. My husband, Shinichiro, sits across from me, gobbling down a plate of bacon and eggs.

Will you listen to this? We've been married for fifty years.

Yesterday, at the Taronga Zoo, a newlywed young lady said to us, 'Your destinies must be connected by the red thread of fate if you've got along for the past fifty years,' and it was then that it occurred to me, *Oh, yes, fifty years*. How deeply moving. It's astonishing really. When I think about it, our honeymoon was just an overnight trip to Atami. Shinichiro was always busy with work, so this is our first trip abroad together. Our daughter gifted us this Sydney trip for our golden anniversary. Yes, there couldn't be a happier occasion.

We were blessed with one daughter. Her name is Hiroko, written 尋子 in kanji characters. But in kindergarten, when I wrote her name in katakana – ヒ (hi) ロ (ro) コ(ko) – next to the kanji, I made the 'ro' too small, and it ended up looking like ピコ, Piko, which sounds like a small bird's chirp. Then everyone started calling her 'Peep'. Isn't that cute? So I call her Peep, too.

To be honest, I wanted more children, but it seems that the stork in charge of our family got lost. Just when we were about to give up, there was finally a knock on our door. I was thirty-six years old when Peep was delivered to us. Now, Peep is thirty-six. It feels strange to think she's the same age as I was then. If we could time-travel and meet as thirty-six-year-olds, what would we talk about? We might even have become best friends. As I watched her grow, I've often thought I love her not just as my daughter but for who she is as a person.

Apparently, Peep was diligently saving up for the past decade or so to gift us a trip abroad for our golden anniversary. Tugs at your heartstrings, doesn't it? Two years ago, Atsuko, a childhood friend of hers, got married in Sydney. When Peep attended the wedding, she did some sightseeing and thought it was just wonderful. If we were to travel, she said it had to be Sydney. She was working for a fashion brand at the

A HALF-CENTURY ROMANCE

time, but she was just starting to consider going off on her own. Now, she has her own lingerie store. I must say, my daughter is quite impressive.

Oh yes, Peep's store is located along a river. Just a little past it, across the bridge, there's a cosy little coffee shop called Marble Cafe. A cute young man named Wataru works there. I imagine that if I'd had a son, he might be like him. Over many conversations, we've become quite good friends.

The other day, when I was at the Marble Cafe, Wataru asked me, 'Do you know what "cherry blossom of the autumn" is?' See, gardening is my hobby, so he must have assumed I know about plants. I think it might refer to the cosmos flower. I told him that the kanji characters for cosmos were 'autumn' and 'cherry blossom'. He said, 'I see,' but his expression suggested otherwise.

They'd set up a Christmas tree in the cafe where people could write their wish on a strip of paper and hang it on the tree, kind of like the bamboo at the Tanabata Star Festival. Apparently, a customer simply wrote 'cherry blossom of the autumn' on their strip. From the look on Wataru's face, I knew immediately that the customer must surely be someone he has feelings for.

Do you know what a 'cherry blossom of the autumn' is? It sounds like a riddle, doesn't it?

I silently watch Shinichiro spread a brown paste on his toast. It's from a yellow packet next to the jam.

'What's this? Chocolate?'

There's something on the packet in English, but I have no idea what it says.

Shinichiro takes a big bite out of it, and his face suddenly contorts. Yes, this is exactly the reaction I was waiting for. I giggle. I had made the same mistake. I expected it to be sweet, but it tasted salty and strange. I didn't like it at all. But as they say, there's no harm in trying. I wanted Shinichiro to try it without any foreknowledge, so I purposely didn't tell him.

I gave up after one bite, but Shinichiro is determinedly taking a second bite, then a third.

'I was surprised at first because it wasn't what I expected, but now I'm used to it, I find the flavour quite interesting.'

Nothing can bring Shinichiro down. He even pulls out his notebook and jots down the white letters on the red banner on the yellow label. VEGEMITE.

'Be-ge-mee-te?'

Shinichiro tilts his head, perplexed. Oh, Peep might have said something about this – that there's a food product that looks like chocolate but is actually salty. If I remember correctly, she called it Vegemite. Yes, looks sweet but is actually salty – isn't that what life is like?

A HALF-CENTURY ROMANCE

I feel reassured when I watch Shinichiro eat a meal. He cherishes every bite of food. No matter how tough things may be, when he's eating, he smiles and savours his meal. We may have many problems, but if we can gratefully enjoy our daily meals, things will work out somehow. When I think of that, I feel energized.

How many times have we shared a meal like this before? And how many more meals do we have left?

Ours was a love marriage, you could say. I worked in accounting at the civil engineering office where Shinichiro was also employed. There were about twelve employees. I was the only woman in the office, so I received quite a bit of attention. I say I worked in accounting, but I did everything. I served everyone's tea, of course, but I also cleaned, ran errands and sometimes even made countless rice balls for the team. How should I put it? It felt like I was the manager of a sports team. Looking back, that was the springtime of my life.

Shinichiro was very serious, and due to his small stature and unassertive nature, he didn't stand out much. Even when someone took credit for his hard-earned achievements, he would smile quietly in the corner. It irritated me. 'Why won't you stand up for yourself more?' I once told him half angrily. He replied, 'I couldn't have done it on my own, and at the end of the day, if it's profitable for the company, it doesn't matter who gets credit.' *This man is never going to get promoted*, I thought. At the time, I was drawn to bold, confident people, and I was dating Yosuke, a large, loud guy at the office who often took on leadership roles. I was convinced we were going to get married.

But Yosuke was our CEO's favourite, and it was arranged he would marry the CEO's daughter. It sounds like the plot of a cheap soap opera, but I was tossed aside without a second thought.

I cried and cried and cried. Even though I didn't do anything wrong, it became difficult for me to work there. Just when I was about to tender my resignation letter, Shinichiro spoke to me. 'Let's get married,' he said.

Not 'Let's start dating', but 'Let's get married'. I thought he felt sorry for me, and it made me want to say something mean. 'There's nothing fun about being with a boring guy like you. I'm attracted to cool guys.' My heart was clouded at the time, so I felt the urge to hurt the gentle Shinichiro. But Shinichiro didn't seem hurt at all. Instead, he smiled and said, 'I'll become cool. I promise you. You might think I'm boring now, but as I age, I'm going to become a handsome silver fox.'

I stood there stunned, observing Shinichiro's

smiling face. Then I imagined it – Shinichiro ageing into an old man. I was surprised by how easily the image came to mind. This man is really going to become a silver fox. If I'm with this person, I will never be unhappy. It quickly transformed from a simple image to a conviction.

So then I resigned from the office and became Shinichiro's bride. Ten years later, when the CEO fell ill, it wasn't Yosuke but Shinichiro who was asked to take over the company. Things hadn't gone well between Yosuke and the CEO's daughter. Not three years into their marriage, his gambling and womanizing led to their divorce. Of course, he quit the company, and no one knew where he went. I heard the CEO's daughter later remarried, this time to someone she loved and unrelated to the company.

After the CEO died, Shinichiro searched desperately for Yosuke. He finally found him, just getting by as a day labourer, and Shinichiro humbly asked if he'd join him in rebuilding the company. At the time, the company was doing well, and there wasn't any need to beg for Yosuke's help, but Shinichiro had been worrying about Yosuke all this time. He knew if he'd simply offered Yosuke a job, Yosuke's pride would have been shattered. Yosuke, for his part, likely understood. He bowed. 'I need your help, too.' With the addition of Yosuke, the company became even more lively and continued to grow significantly. But Shinichiro never changes. He's humble and modest, and he's always smiling. He doesn't grovel to anyone, regardless of their importance, and he also doesn't act superior towards newcomers. I think humility is true confidence, and genuine kindness is strength.

It was about five years ago that I suddenly noticed: *Oh, Shinichiro's hair has turned grey . . . no, a beautiful silver*.

Having finished his breakfast, Shinichiro calls over to the server and asks, 'Can I have a coffee refill, please?'

He seems relieved that there's Japanese staff here. The young server, with her long black hair tied back, responds with a cheerful, 'Absolutely.' The bright green bracelet around her wrist looks great on her. I might have been around her age when I first met Shinichiro. I can see myself offering him a teacup, saying, 'Please have some tea.'

'Shinichiro, you weren't lying,' I say.

Shinichiro blinks twice and lets out a chuckle.

'About what?'

I've been rambling on, haven't I? I'm sorry to have made you listen to me the whole time you've been eating. You must be hungry. Would you like some bread?

I'm about to offer a piece of bread when the server returns with a pot of coffee.

'That bird's called a lorikeet. Isn't it vibrantly coloured?'

A blue face, orange chest and green wings. A ring of yellow around its neck like a scarf. It's truly bursting with colour.

Suddenly, Shinichiro says, 'Misako, how beautiful.'

Oh my! The unexpected compliment makes my heart sing like a harp, and I feel like a young girl again. It's been decades since Shinichiro has spoken to me like that – no, come to think of it, I don't recall him ever saying anything like that, even when we were newlyweds. I'm so overjoyed and embarrassed. I bite my lower lip and look up, only to find Shinichiro's gaze fixed on the lorikeet.

When he said 'how beautiful', did he mean me or the lorikeet?

Oh, well. As I look between the brightly coloured lorikeet and the gently smiling Shinichiro, I think to myself that Shinichiro's romantic silver is even more lovely.

7

The Countdown

Green

When I'm asked why I came to Australia and I answer, 'To paint green,' people don't know quite how to react.

'Oh, I see,' some say and end the conversation right there. Others probe relentlessly for deeper reasons. I also get a lot of 'When you say green, you mean plants, right?' and when I answer, 'No, I mean the colour,' they tilt their heads in confusion, asking, 'What do you mean "the colour"?' It seems people don't quite understand me, but it's the colour green that I love.

Sometimes, there are people who grasp this immediately. Not long ago, when I told a lady dining at the hotel restaurant where I work that I came to Australia to paint green, she said, 'Oh, you're an artist, then.' Not at all, I protested. I'm not an artist. I just paint for fun. She smiled and said, 'No, if you paint, you're an artist. It doesn't matter if you're paid for it or not.'

The woman was here with her husband, and they looked like a happy, close couple. I remember them mentioning that their daughter had gifted them a trip to Sydney for their golden anniversary. I've never considered myself an artist, but when I hear a woman with a wealth of life experience call me this, I start to feel like maybe I am.

It's New Year's Eve today, and the weather is perfect.

In Sydney, there's a free newspaper for Japanese expats called *CANVAS*. I've been interviewed for a story on my working holiday experience for its website. I don't often read that kind of magazine, but since the interview, I've started picking up every issue.

I especially like Maco's column. It features topics such as differences in Japanese and Australian culture and tips on the English language. This month, the column covers New Year's celebrations.

According to the column, here, spectacular fireworks are set off over the Sydney Harbour Bridge right after the countdown. A multitude of fireworks fill the sky at once, and their reflections shimmer on the water, lighting up the entire place. I learned from the article that the spectators who gather there kiss at midnight.

But this has nothing to do with me. I plan to spend

THE COUNTDOWN

New Year's Eve at my apartment. I don't have anyone to kiss, and I'm not into kissing strangers.

I head to the Royal Botanic Garden with my sketchbook and paints as always. The grounds are vast, and if you are serious about exploring, you'll need to spend a good half-day there. It's filled with lush trees and rollicking blooms. Bats hang from branches, and a red tourist tram chugs through the park. It's hard to believe such a beautiful place exists in the middle of a business area.

On my way here, I swung by my favourite sandwich shop and picked up a chicken sandwich and lemonade for 'takeaway'. The 'takeout' that I learned at school is American English. The usual man in the orange apron greeted me with an Australian-accented 'G'day!' and gave me a thumbs-up and a wink.

To withstand the mid-summer sun, a hat and sunglasses are essential. But I'll take them off when I'm sitting at the foot of a giant tree; that's when my time of bliss begins.

I take a sip of lemonade. My skin scorches under the sun, but the moment I step into the shade of a tree, I am embraced by a coolness as though it had been waiting for my arrival. All I can see is the invigorating blue of the Sydney Harbour. Fully content, I open my sketchbook.

I squeeze paint on to palette paper – yellow and blue. I create, spread and paint green freely, savouring the sensation of each brushstroke as I inhale the park's air and the scent of the trees and the paint. I watch my world become immersed in green. *Ahh, what bliss.*

'. . . this?'

A voice snaps me back to reality. A slender young guy with smooth brown hair has appeared beside me. He is leaning in and peering into my face.

'Huh?'

'Did you drop this?'

He holds out a handkerchief and smiles shyly.

I let my guard down.

'Oh, thank you. It's mine.'

I quickly stand and take the handkerchief. I used it to wipe my forehead earlier while walking. I thought I'd tucked it into the side pocket of my backpack.

When I thank him again, he flashes a brilliant smile and nods.

. . . Green?

I can't believe my eyes. I'm not psychic, nor do I know anything about that, but I see what people might call his 'aura'. Even though he's wearing a white T-shirt, I see his body swathed in a soft green glow.

As I stand in bewilderment, he glances down at my sketchbook and says, 'You're an artist, aren't you?'

THE COUNTDOWN

For some reason, I answer, 'Yes.' Maybe it's because of what the lady at the hotel said to me.

'I thought so! Will you show me your work?' He crouches down near my sketchbook and admires my green, even though it hasn't dried yet.

I don't know why, but I feel content. I sit down and watch him and the green.

'So you don't use green paint?' he asks, his eyes gripped by the pages of my sketchbook.

'Exactly. It's *my* green.'

I use yellow and blue as the base, then gradually mix in different colours.

I don't know when it began. I remember already being like this at kindergarten, so maybe I was born this way. The colour green has always enchanted me. It's a feeling too intense to simply describe as my 'liking' it. Green is my friend, my talisman, my memory, my future. It soothes me, and it energizes me. Even when I didn't get along with my classmates, I never felt alone when I had the colour green. What dogs or cats or music or books are for some people, green has always been for me.

That's why I always keep green close to me.

When working at the hotel, I wear a chartreuse-green bracelet to stay energized and active. When I sleep, I use a deep green pillowcase to help calm my body and heart. The handkerchief I always use is the colour of new leaves.

Sundries, stationery, furniture – I always look at the green options first. But not every green item will do. Some greens don't sit well with me, and there are many that I think are OK, but not quite what I'm looking for. That's why I started trying to create my own green.

During my second year of junior college, a gallery in my hometown of Kyoto hosted a free exhibition. The exhibition didn't feature famous works but showed what the gallery owner personally liked. When I went in, I stopped instinctively before an acrylic painting.

It was a painting of lush vegetation – it possessed a fearless vitality, but beneath the surface, there was also an inescapable fragility and melancholy. The trees looked like they were dancing, and the leaves looked like they were singing. The green drew me in.

'That's a botanic garden in Sydney. A friend painted it.'

When I turned around, an unassuming older man stood behind me. He seemed to be the gallery owner. He was short and had a large mole in the centre of his forehead.

I looked at the painting. The green was certainly saying to me, 'Come to Sydney. It's waiting for you.'

THE COUNTDOWN

'You should visit,' said the man with the mole. He took a business card from his breast pocket, and on its back, he wrote down the name of the garden – 'Royal Botanic Garden'. I'd not said a single word, but he appeared to understand completely. Only the word MAESTRO was printed on his business card. There was no phone number or email address.

A single painting can transform a person's life – I believe this.

The moment I stepped into the long-awaited garden, I felt as if I heard someone say, 'We've been waiting for you.' Oh, this place overflowed with my green. I felt welcomed. This was the first time I felt that green loved me back. That's why opening my sketchbook at the botanic garden is kind of like going on a 'date' with the colour green. I can't admit this to anyone, of course.

Date. I suddenly become aware again of the young man with the kind smile who appeared out of nowhere. He's maybe in his late twenties. He could be younger; he could be older.

'I want to see the others, too. Show me?'

He's taken on a more familiar tone. I've never shown my sketchbook to anyone. But I feel I can show him.

'Sure, go ahead,' I say, but he hands the sketchbook back to me.

Instead of sitting across from each other, we sit side by side and trace my greens.

Place. Season. Time. The greens I've observed, the greens I've imagined. Coloured pencils, pastels, paint. The shapes of leaves, circles, squares, geometric patterns; some filled solidly, lightened with water, stippled. My green. Green and me.

'Is "You" your name?' he asks, looking at my signature in the corner of a piece.

'Yeah.'

My name is You, written with the kanji character, 優. With its many strokes, it's challenging to write the character evenly, so I took to writing 'You' in small, cursive English letters.

'*You*. It feels like you're addressing me. I like it. I'm sure people often tell you they would like to have this painting.'

'No, never. I've never exhibited my work. I paint for myself.'

Now I feel a little embarrassed that I agreed when he called me an artist earlier.

His face is so close to mine that I can almost touch it, but I can't bring myself to look at him. He's probably smiling. I keep my gaze down. 'You're not going to ask?'

'Ask what?'

'Why I paint only green?'

THE COUNTDOWN

'Do you need a reason for that?'

He adjusts his seat. It's a simple gesture, but it's clear he has shifted his position so we can talk more easily.

'And you say "only green", but within the shade, there are so many tones. To me, they all look distinct. Each one is lovely. Happiness, joy, loneliness, anger, affection, passion – I feel them all. I hope you keep painting more and more green,' he replies gently but firmly.

'So, I can carry on being like I am?'

I'm surprised by the words that drop out of my mouth. The door that I thought was closed seems to have swung open. The words I've been holding back begin to tumble out.

So, I can continue painting green like this?

My mother always used to say, *Why can't you be normal like the other kids? You keep drawing green pictures and collecting green things. It's weird, pointless. Something must be wrong with you.* When I was in the fifth grade, my homeroom teacher said that I should get a psychiatric evaluation, and from then on, my mother never smiled at me again. The precious greens I had painted were torn and thrown away. But I couldn't bring myself to say, 'Stop.' It felt like I had been torn apart and thrown into the trash. I could only watch, my heart hardening, without shedding a single tear. I thought my mother's word was the law. *You need to be more like your brother. He excels at school. You're such a disappointment. How can I love a daughter who can't make friends and only draws things like this?*

That's why I wanted to leave home when I graduated from junior college. I wanted to get as far away as possible. I was truly happy that the painting of the botanic garden – this green – called out to me. It might just be something my desperate desire conjured up, but it was what saved me. But in three months, my visa expires. What should I do when I return to Japan?

After a long silence, he exhales. He gently places his hand on my head.

'You've experienced some difficult things.'

Pat pat. He taps me on the crown of my head twice, then envelops me in an embrace.

'Despite all that, you couldn't stop painting, right? You couldn't stop loving green. That's because you're an artist.'

He drops his arms and holds my hand.

'That's why you need to keep painting. There are people who will be saved by your green. You are drawing "you" – yourself, the artist – and also "you" – the viewer. Each person will surely find a piece to connect with. Get your work out there.'

I begin to cry. I cry like an infant who hasn't yet learned words. I cry and cry and cry. I cry out loud. I

shatter the heavy and unyielding thing that I've been clinging to, pretending it was important and that I needed it. Deep down, I knew it all along – I wanted to let it go.

Now, at last, I'm truly free.

He squeezes my hand with a gentle pressure before planting a gentle kiss on my forehead.

He is a stranger, but I don't mind it at all. In fact, I feel like I've known him for a long time. But I'm so embarrassed, I can't look him in the eye.

There's still some time before the countdown, but I've already received an early New Year's kiss.

He lets go of my hand. 'Thank you.'

For loving me.

Perhaps it's a trick of the ear, but that's what I think I heard.

I wipe my tear-soaked cheeks with the handkerchief he picked up. I am starting to feel like myself again. Realizing I haven't asked him his name, I look up.

But there's no one there – only the wind gently rustling the lush green leaves of the trees.

8

Ralph's Best Day

Orange

There's a small sandwich shop near the botanic garden. Its orange awning and sign are emblazoned with 'Ralph's Kitchen' in white letters. Ralph is the shop owner's name.

Every morning, Ralph dons his orange apron and hums as he prepares for the day. Ham, lettuce, tomato, smoked salmon. He adds a generous dollop of mayonnaise and a tiny bit of mustard to the chopped-up boiled eggs. *Who will come by today?* Basking in the morning sun, he pictures the day's customers with trembling excitement.

Ralph might look a little older than his age. Nearing forty, he has a round belly, thinning hair and a love for silly jokes. He greets every customer with a loud 'G'day!' and a wink. An Australian 'Good day!' serves as both a 'hello' and a wish for a lovely day. Recipients of his greeting can't help but feel uplifted, as if they've just recovered from a cold. Maybe it's because he makes you feel that he genuinely cherishes even the briefest interaction with you. Ralph's sunny smile is always full of heart.

Ralph doesn't have a wife. Or a lover . . . though, there was once a woman he cared for. Despite his cheerful disposition, he is incredibly shy when it comes to women. He never managed to tell the woman how he felt before they lost touch, and that was the end of it.

Ralph is skilled at household chores, so living alone is not a problem for him. But when beautiful flowers bloom on his balcony, and he has no one to whom he can turn and say, 'Look at that,' he feels a pang of loneliness.

Ralph's Kitchen was originally a bakery run by Ralph's father, which he has since renovated. After graduating from college, Ralph began working at a bank, but about three years ago, his father decided to open a much larger bakery in the centre of the city, so Ralph quit his job at the bank and took over this store.

Ralph didn't dislike the meticulous counting and managing of money at his old job. But now, whether it's becoming friends with his customers or thinking things like, *Today's tomatoes are glossy and beautiful*, or preparing extra lemonade on a particularly hot day, or wondering if he should change the design on the

RALPH'S BEST DAY

napkins, he finds immense joy in work driven not by numbers but by how he feels. Of course, his experience in banking has been very helpful with billing and managing the store's finances.

Orange is Ralph and the store's signature colour. There's a bit of a story here.

Three years ago, when Ralph was still working for the bank, he fell in love with Cindy, a beautiful and intelligent woman who lived in the apartment unit next to his. She was fifteen years his junior, and he had no idea what she did for work. But whenever Cindy opened her front door or when both their windows were open on a hot day, a gentle, sweet scent drifted over. When Ralph caught a whiff of that scent, he was filled with peace and couldn't help but blissfully close his eyes. Was the scent flowers, perfume or fruit? It seemed like it could be any of those, yet none of them – it was truly enchanting. But whenever he ran into Cindy by the entranceway or on the street, he couldn't bring himself to ask her. Instead, he resorted to telling silly jokes to make her laugh.

One winter morning, as Ralph was leaving his apartment to go to work, he bumped into Cindy retying her bootlaces.

'Good morning, Ralph!'

She looked up at him from her crouched position, her face breaking into a smile as clear as a blooming lotus.

Ralph became so flustered that he was barely able to squeak, 'You're heading out early today, aren't you?'

'Yes, I'm taking the bus. Are you going for the train?'

Cindy rose, and they naturally began walking side by side. At first, Ralph tried to say something witty, but he gradually grew embarrassed and looked down in silence. To lighten the mood, Cindy said, 'Here's a personality test. What's your favourite colour?'

The sudden question caught him off guard. But as if drawn in by the soft scent that tickled his nose, he answered without thinking, 'Orange.'

'Why?'

There was nothing quite as cute as Cindy with her head tilted. He couldn't help but smile. 'Because it's a fun colour. It's not as assertive as red, and it's not as eccentric as yellow. It's warm and inviting and fills people with energy and cheer.'

Cindy blinked for a moment. 'Yes, you're right,'

she said. 'Your favourite colour is supposed to represent your "ideal self". It's actually not so much the colour you choose but your reason for picking it. But, Ralph, your reason for picking orange, rather than representing your "ideal self", is who you already are.'

She sounded satisfied with her conclusion. Ralph racked his brain for a response but couldn't find the words. His mind raced, and beads of sweat formed on his forehead. Before he knew it, they had arrived at the bus stop.

Cindy joined the line for the bus, and Ralph, reluctant to leave, stood silently beside her. Soon, the bus arrived. *I have to say something. Something.* But it was Cindy who spoke up in a small but firm voice. 'Orange will be your signature.'

Signature? What did she mean?

'See you later, Mr Orange!'

Without waiting for his reply, Cindy boarded the bus and left. It wasn't until the following week that he heard from other residents that she had moved away, leaving him no chance to reply.

Less than six months later, Ralph decided to open his sandwich shop. Around the same time, it was announced that the apartment building would be demolished. It was, after all, a very old structure.

When Ralph heard the news, a wave of sadness washed over him. If Cindy came back, how would she know where to find him? The apartment building was the one connection between them.

He was full of regret. He shouldn't have been so shy. He should have talked to her more. Even if his feelings were unreciprocated, he should have told her he liked her. If he could see her again, he would make sure to tell her how he felt.

But he quickly reassured himself, 'It's OK.' He decided to make orange – as Cindy foretold – the signature colour of his shop.

Choosing orange for the awning, sign and apron was the right decision. Locals refer to the shop not as 'Ralph's Kitchen' but as the 'Orange Shop'. Ralph welcomes that. He is proud that the colour orange and not the shop's name has become his hallmark. The thought that hungry people come to his shop, drawn by the bright orange, fills his heart with so much joy that he feels as if he's sprouted wings and is soaring through the skies.

It's all thanks to Cindy.

RALPH'S BEST DAY

Once he's finished tidying up after closing, he settles at the counter and shuts his eyes as he reminisces about her. As he pictures Cindy's long, ivy-like hair and her fair, supple skin that looks like it might bounce at the slightest touch, a gentle smile appears on his face.

He thinks he smells a familiar, tenderly sweet scent. He closes his eyes and takes a deep breath.

'I found it.'

Oh, I'm even hearing things today . . . He chuckles to himself and slowly opens his eyes.

Cindy stands before him, looking a bit more grown-up than when he last saw her three years ago. She has suddenly appeared, like a figure in a music box.

'Long time no see, Ralph.'

'Cindy? Is it really you? I can't believe it.'

'It really is me. I've been in England, but I arrived back in Sydney yesterday.'

There are many things he wants to say to her, but he asks her the question he is second most curious about.

'What's your favourite colour?'

She answers without hesitation as if she knew he was going to ask. 'Turquoise.'

'Why?'

'Because it's mysterious and feels like it has

magical power. It can make you wait for me in the orange and welcome me back with a smile.'

Ah, turquoise. That's lovely. It's exactly Cindy. She draws closer and playfully tugs at the hem of his apron.

'Do you think my magic spell worked?'

Without thinking, he pulls her into a tight embrace before shyness can overtake him.

'It worked. It worked almost too well.'

Cindy lifts her face ever so slightly. She smiles as if she's won a gold medal, before nestling her head into his chest.

Cindy's scent seems to permeate Ralph's being. He can't tell if he's crying or laughing, but he squeezes her once more and says, 'Don't ever undo your spell, OK?'

The evening sun streams in through the window. *Good day, Ralph.* It will be a while before he notices the orange bathing them both as if bestowing a blessing.

9

The Return of the Witch

Turquoise

I've always wanted to be a witch. I've known ever since I was learning the alphabet in kindergarten. I had no idea how to become a witch, and no one would teach me how, but I believed I could become one someday.

I thought, with practice, I could learn to fly on a broomstick or move things with the wave of a wand, but I was particularly drawn to concocting potions. Alone in a dark room, I crushed wildflowers and berries and mixed them to my liking while I imagined their potential effects. Once, the night before my school's field day, I prepared and drank my masterpiece, 'Race-enhancing potion', and upset my stomach. My mother scolded me harshly. Lying in bed, I admitted my mistake, and my mother stroked my cheek. 'As long as you've learned your lesson.' She probably thought I'd never do it again. But as I rubbed my stomach, I thought, *The way I brewed it was wrong. I'll get it right the next time.*

It was Ms Grace who first ignited my interest. On an elementary school hiking trip, she accompanied our class as a special guide. She was researching botany at the university and taught us the names of flowers and identified which berries were safe to eat.

During our hike, one of my classmates stumbled on a rock and scraped their knee. Ms Grace quickly disappeared into the woods and returned with a handful of leaves. She crumpled the leaves, pressed them against the wound, and murmured, 'Chichin puipui.' *Chichin puipui*. Her funny-sounding words had us all in stitches. Seeing my injured classmate stop crying and start to laugh, I thought, *It's magic. Ms Grace is a witch.*

I couldn't stop laughing but for a very different reason than the others. I didn't take my eyes off Ms Grace for the rest of the hike. I was still giggling while unpacking our lunchboxes, which creeped out my friends.

Ms Grace stood with perfect posture. Her earlobes, which peeked out from beneath her loosely tied hair, were adorned with beautiful stone earrings. After we got back from the hike, I approached her.

'Ms Grace, may I ask you a question?'

'Of course. What is it, Cindy?'

I was surprised she remembered my name even though I'd only said it once during initial introductions.

'What kind of leaf was that?'

'Oh!' Ms Grace winked. 'It's a magical leaf that heals injuries.'

I knew it!

Thrilled, I fired off another question. 'What about that funny word you said?'

'You mean "chichin puipui"? My Japanese friend taught me that. It's a spell that transforms the world into a wonderful place. Cute, isn't it?'

'Very!' I took a deep breath and mustered my courage to ask, 'Ms Grace, are you a witch?'

She looked at me for a moment, then pressed an index finger to her lips. 'Shh, it's a secret,' she whispered.

I jumped in delight, but unfortunately I never saw Ms Grace again. After that, a different teacher accompanied us on extracurricular activities and camping trips. I wanted to learn more magic from Ms Grace, and I deeply regretted not asking for her contact information.

From then on, I read every plant encyclopedia I could find. I discovered that many plants have antiseptic and haemostatic properties. But that wasn't all. Plants also possess the power – the magic – to heal people. With my heart pounding with excitement, I devoured botany books and became obsessed with visiting botanic gardens.

And another thing: I soon learned that the stones that adorned Ms Grace's ears were called turquoise. I found a necklace with the same stone in the window of an antique store. Through the glass, I recited the word on the label – turquoise – several times. From my research, I found out that turquoise was a mysterious stone. It had been used in magic and rituals since ancient times and cherished by people as protective amulets. It was also believed to be connected to spirits and the cosmos. So, I began to like turquoise and wear it . . . in order to become a witch. Turquoise became my chosen colour.

In high school, a Japanese exchange student joined my class. Maco was in Sydney just for a year. When Maco saw my turquoise bracelet, she said, 'What a beautiful colour. In Japanese, it's called "mizuiro".'

She wrote the word in her notebook and taught me that 'mizu' meant water. 'Mizuiro'. The colour of water. Now that I think about it, in English, there's the shade 'aqua'. In the colourless, transparent water, we inevitably see mysterious colour.

'Then, do you know about "chichin puipui'? I asked.

Maco laughed in delight.

'Every Japanese person knows it. It's the most powerful spell there is.'

If that's the case, all Japanese people must be magical. It was no wonder Ms Grace had a Japanese friend, I thought.

My interest in plants naturally led me to aromatherapy. My certification textbook described how, in medieval Europe, those skilled in using medicinal herbs and spices were often ostracized as witches. I reflected on this sorrowful history and felt it was my duty to carry on the tradition left behind by the witches who came before me. Immediately after graduating high school, I got my aromatherapy certification and started working as an instructor at an aromatherapy salon. Teaching students who shared my eagerness to learn about the power of plants was deeply rewarding.

Five or so years into working at the salon, I was doing some research online when I came upon something by chance: Ms Grace was teaching at an aromatherapy school in England. This was about three years ago. All I had to go on was one picture from that hiking trip years ago and her name, but I was sure it was her. When I emailed the aromatherapy school to enquire, Ms Grace herself responded, inviting me to join her at the school. And just like that, I quit the salon and left for England.

My only regret was that I'd fallen in love with my neighbour, Ralph.

Ralph was fifteen years my senior and worked at a bank. He was a bit chubby, short and had thinning hair – these seemed to be insecurities for him, but I found them endearing. His roundish body was packed with affection that spilled into his smile. Just looking at him made me feel at ease. His balcony was filled with lovingly tended flowers, and the appetizing aroma of home-cooked meals wafted from his apartment at dinner time. He was the kind of person who would go out of his way to help a lost old lady, making her laugh with silly jokes until he'd seen her safely to her destination.

I didn't want him to be with anyone else, but I couldn't tell him that. I also couldn't tell him I was leaving Sydney because I didn't know when I'd be back.

So, instead, I put a spell on him.

Just before I left for England, I finally perfected the love potion I'd been working on for a while. Oil of ylang-ylang, essence of lotus, forget-me-not petals, my sigh, a drop of moonlight . . . *the rest is a secret*. I mixed them all into a special rose water and sprayed the potion generously on myself from head to toe. Then I waited for him in our building's lobby to catch him leaving for work. I pretended it was a chance meeting and got him to walk me to the bus stop.

I asked him silly questions like, 'What's your favourite colour?' I tossed my hair and tilted my head, doing my best to send the potion's essence his way. When he said he liked the colour orange, such an adorably fitting answer for him, my heart skipped a beat. Then, all of a sudden, as if I were watching a movie trailer, an image appeared before my eyes: Ralph wearing an orange apron and happily making sandwiches. It disappeared within a few seconds, but I knew then that he might be a banker now, but he was going to become a sandwich shop owner. It was the first time I'd experienced something like that, but I wasn't surprised. Some part of me knew that anyone truly in love could wield this kind of magic.

When I return to Sydney, I'll look for the orange sandwich shop.

Please wait for me, Ralph.

As we parted ways, I called him 'Mr Orange', sealing the future I'd just glimpsed. And as I boarded the bus, I discreetly cast a 'chichin puipui' spell to lock in the enchantment.

In England, I was reunited with Ms Grace, and I threw myself even deeper into the study of aromatherapy. Ms Grace remembered me well, and she taught me many things both at school and outside class. We volunteered at medical clinics and participated in forest conservation activities, and through assisting Ms Grace, I learned first hand how people, flora and fauna interact and support each other. All that breathes on this Earth is interconnected. To know this, to reflect on it, to feel it, to wish for it and to put it into action – these were the essentials to mastering Ms Grace's magic.

When I received my programme completion certificate, Ms Grace said, 'You're a fully fledged witch now, Cindy.'

Magic that transforms the world into a wonderful place – I can apply this to so many things. To return the smiles to the faces of the sick, to disarm hateful hearts with embraces, to bestow gentle dreams upon sleepless nights.

Having completed my training in England, I'm about to start a new life in Sydney. With turquoise in hand, aromatherapy at the ready and 'chichin puipui' on my lips, I will brighten the world. And I'll be doing it all by the side of my charming lover, who wears a sunny orange apron.

10

If I Hadn't Met You

Black

I start to write 'made his eyes black and white', a Japanese idiom for blinking in surprise, when I let out an 'Ah!' I'm in the middle of translating an English picture book for a publisher, and the main character is a blue-eyed westerner. I wanted to express his shock, but to say this blue-eyed character made his eyes black and white would be absurd.

This means the line 'I won't allow it "while my eyes are still black"', an idiom that means 'as long as I'm alive', also won't work. I let out a sigh and grin. I have to tell Grace about this – she loves Japanese.

At thirty-six, I still marvel at how humans – creatures with the same basic form, though we may vary in size and colour – can speak such different languages while sharing the same planet. Life would be simpler if only we could understand each other's languages. Still, I'm grateful that God made human communication just a bit complicated. It's given me the joy of translation – of absorbing both English and Japanese, transforming the words into mine, and sending them back out into the world.

I began dreaming of becoming a translator when I was around fourteen. Though I'd never even left Tokyo's Shitamachi area, I loved foreign children's literature, and English was the only class I enjoyed at school. I wanted to pursue literary translation, engaging deeply with a text on my own, rather than interpretation, which required public speaking and quick thinking.

This desire was further fuelled by my meeting with Grace.

In middle school, I joined the English club. One day, our club's advisor brought a list of pen pals from our sister school abroad as part of an international exchange programme. I found the idea of exchanging letters with someone I didn't know from a foreign country deeply romantic. My heart raced as I scanned the list. It included countries, names, ages, and brief introductory messages. America, Canada, Singapore. I carefully read each line.

Grace from Australia. Fourteen years old. 'I can talk with flowers.'

Her self-introduction mesmerized me. What an interesting thing to say. There was no one like her around me.

The many letters I exchanged with Grace enriched my childhood. Grace could truly communicate with flowers and trees. She not only understood when they needed water or weren't getting enough sunlight, but they'd also tell her things like if it was going to rain the next day, as well as enjoying casual chit-chat. Grace constantly talked to the plants, telling them about her fight with her mother, her crush on a boy, her new Japanese pen pal (me); and in her letters, she told me how they'd responded.

How wonderful, I thought. She could decipher the language of plants, a language unknown to me, and relate it in her own words. It was a form of 'translation'. I enjoyed reading her translations, but I'm sure it was even more fun for Grace.

Grace's connection with plants continued into adulthood. She neither allowed herself to become overwhelmed nor arrogant about her abilities. She gratefully harnessed the blessings bestowed upon her by the plants and improved people's lives through aromatherapy and herbology.

After years of writing letters, we finally met when I was twenty. I visited Sydney during my college summer break. Grace came to pick me up at the airport, and the moment she saw me, she exclaimed, 'Such dark eyes. How lovely!' repeatedly. Japanese people were not that rare in Sydney, but Grace couldn't stop admiring my dark eyes. Her own eyes, a clear light brown, were also very beautiful.

'The black of your irises is different from anyone else's, Atsuko. There's no cloudiness in them. That's why they reflect everything so clearly. You can see things others might not even notice.'

Until then, I'd neither liked nor disliked my eyes. But Grace's words made me feel like I, too, might have some special power, and it gave me courage.

After graduating from college with a degree in English, I landed a position at a small translation company. My role primarily involved translating manuals for imported goods and machinery. It was a respectable translation job, and it wasn't that I wasn't proud of it – but it was literature that I wanted to translate. I wanted to publish books as a translator.

The path to literary translation was challenging. I entered every literary translation contest I came across but never won. An occasional honourable mention didn't lead to a career.

No matter how many times I failed, I never got used to the sting. With each submission, I thought, *This time, for sure.* Yet my mailed manuscripts became scrap paper, and the ones I'd submitted online vanished as if they'd never existed, taking my time, effort and dreams with them. Whenever I read the

winning entries, I sighed and wondered what set them apart from mine.

Even so, Grace believed in my becoming a literary translator even more steadfastly than I did. She often said, 'Your dream is going to come true. You're going to be a brilliant translator. I guarantee it.' I can't describe how much those words encouraged me. If Grace said so, then maybe it was true. And by believing her, I was able to find hope in my own future.

On one of my annual visits to Sydney to see Grace, I met Mark, an interior designer. Swept off my feet, we got married rather suddenly five years ago when I was thirty-one. It wasn't so much his passion that moved me, but rather his easy-going 'No worries!' Aussie attitude that won me over. Since I wasn't a huge fan of being the focus of attention, I settled in Sydney without throwing a wedding.

I couldn't find a suitable job right away, so I spent my time at the library for a while. There were many excellent books in Australia that hadn't been translated into Japanese yet, and I devoured them. Overcome by the urge to translate, I transformed the text into my own words and poured them into notebooks with no intention of submitting them anywhere.

HOT CHOCOLATE ON THURSDAY

When I first moved to Sydney, I spent so much time with Grace that even Mark became jealous. But soon after, she left for England to pursue her studies in aromatherapy.

With the rise of email, we seldom send each other airmail any more. Thanks to the internet, I feel as close to Grace as if she were in the same room with me. No matter how many years go by, we never run out of things to talk about. I still open her emails with the same excitement I had at fourteen when I eagerly waited for a letter in the mailbox.

Two years ago, Grace sent me an email. 'I had a dream of you in a wedding dress, surrounded by plants. You must absolutely have your wedding at the botanic garden as soon as possible. It'll open up the world, not just for you, but many people as well.'

Apparently, it was a prophecy from the plants. Being introverted and having made few friends since moving to Sydney, I was unsure. But when I thought about it, having a wedding in Japan would mean dealing with the expectations and obligations of friends and family, which would be even more of a hassle. As an only child, having my parents see me in my wedding dress felt like a meaningful way to honour them, and a destination wedding was a good excuse to invite only close family. I invited four people – my parents, my childhood friend Peep, and Grace – and

we had a modest ceremony at the botanic garden, just as Grace suggested.

A casual wedding with our loved ones was more fun than I'd imagined. Above all, I was thrilled that Grace could be there. At the time, Peep, who was dreaming of opening a store for handcrafted lingerie, was inspired when Grace told her, 'Blue is the colour of the Blessed Virgin Mary.' Someday, Peep said, she was going to make Marian-blue lingerie.

Mark's guests were mostly cheerful Australians, but there was a Japanese man among them. He was probably just over fifty. The mole in the centre of his forehead stood out.

As soon as Mark spotted him, he dashed over to him like a dog to his owner and introduced him to me.

'This is my trusted colleague. We call him "Maestro".'

'Maestro?'

'Yes, because he's a master – he has a master's degree from a university in Australia,' said Mark.

The Maestro laughed.

'That's not the reason, but I do like being called "Maestro".'

He went back and forth between Japan and Sydney and was involved with a swathe of endeavours. He worked with Mark on spatial design for stores and buildings.

'You know that popular sandwich shop that opened last year? You said it was great, remember? We worked on that together.'

I knew it well. It was the orange shop run by a cheerful man.

'Where are you from?' the Maestro asked me in smooth English, likely out of consideration for Mark.

'Tokyo,' I replied.

'Ah! I currently live there, though I'm originally from Kyoto. I have a small art gallery there. Mark, could you paint something for my next show? Your art is far too brilliant to remain just a hobby.'

Mark nodded enthusiastically.

'Absolutely. I'll paint this botanic garden we're at today!'

When the Maestro learned that I was pursuing a career in literary translation, he introduced me to a Japanese publisher without even asking much about my professional background. I was initially assigned to do a rough translation, and an editor who liked my work began periodically sending me projects.

One day, I mustered up my courage and pitched a book I wanted to translate to my editor. Much to my surprise, everything moved forward smoothly, and last month, my translation of an Australian children's book was published in Japan. 'Your streak of bad luck lasted a while, but things are really taking off

for you now,' said Mark. But I think that's not quite right. It wasn't bad luck but rather that becoming a translator required this much time and experience.

My name is on the cover of the book. I've run my finger over it countless times, pressed my cheek to it, inhaled the scent of ink and embraced the book that has come into the world.

Grace was happier for me than anyone else. 'But I knew this was going to happen,' she said. It was true. Grace had been predicting this day since she was fourteen.

I might not have become a translator if I hadn't met her. And I definitely wouldn't be living in Sydney.

March in Sydney is lovely, with the heat finally letting up.

At an outdoor cafe in the Circular Quay, I power on my laptop. I'm typing an email to Grace when I suddenly feel someone's gaze. A young blonde woman at the neighbouring table is watching me. There's writing paper and an envelope in front of her – she appears to be writing a letter. I catch a glimpse of the top of the page and see 'Dearest Maco'.

I smile when our eyes meet, and she flinches in surprise.

'I'm sorry for staring. You remind me of a Japanese friend of mine.'

'Are you writing a letter to that friend?'

'I am. She stayed with my family as a homestay student a long time ago. I know people tend to do everything by email nowadays, but we both like letter-writing.'

'I know what you mean. There's something charming about letters, isn't there?'

She nods softly and turns her gaze to the sea. Beyond the ferries coming and going lies the Sydney Harbour Bridge.

'If I hadn't met her, I might not be alive today,' she says, shaking her blonde head.

I turn to her in surprise, and she lowers her gaze.

'I was sick, but she saved me at a critical moment.'

'Oh, is your friend a doctor?'

'No . . . but we've known each other for a long time, from a past life.'

Past life.

I stare blankly at her. She smiles and tucks the letter set into her bag.

'Thank you for listening to me.'

'Thank *you* for sharing this lovely story.'

I give a slight bow, and the blonde woman departs gracefully.

If there is such a thing as past lives, I'm sure Grace and I have a deep connection as well.

Being obsessed with the English language, I might

have been someone from the English-speaking world, and the Japanophile Grace might have been Japanese. There's no way to know for sure, but the idea makes sense to me.

'Sorry to keep you waiting.'

Mark is here. He had business near by, so we decided to meet at this cafe. He is accompanied by the Maestro. There's a major art and design event happening in Sydney tomorrow, and the Maestro is here for work. Later this evening, there's a pre-event party for everyone involved, and I've been invited to join them.

'I'll grab us some drinks,' says Mark. He leaves the Maestro with me and heads to the back of the cafe.

I rise from my seat and bow. 'It's been a while,' I say in Japanese.

The Maestro gives his usual relaxed smile.

'I read the book you translated. It was great.'

'Thank you so much,' I reply. 'I couldn't have done it without you introducing me to the publisher despite my lack of experience.'

The Maestro scratches his forehead.

'I do have an eye for potential.'

We sit together and gaze out at the sea. He is a curious man who has an absent-minded air about him.

'Do you paint yourself, Maestro?' I ask.

'I don't. My role is to unearth individuals with

immense talent and to spread their work to the world. I love that feeling you get when you're just on the verge of turning your dreams into reality.'

Mark returns with two cappuccinos. We are chatting for a bit when Mark suddenly recalls something: 'We just came from a meeting with a client in Paddington.'

Paddington is a suburb of Sydney. Every Saturday, a large flea market is held in the grounds of a church there.

'I found this painting at the flea market. For some reason, it reminded me of my childhood and brought me to tears. The moment I saw it, I knew I had to buy it. A Japanese girl with long hair was selling it. She had a collection of her work up for sale.'

It's a pale green painting with geometric patterns and soft light that play off each other. In the bottom-right corner, it's signed 'You'.

The Maestro takes the painting and scrutinizes it for a while before saying softly, 'What time does the flea market close?'

'Hmm? I think five o'clock?'

I look at my watch. It's three. Paddington is about fifteen minutes away by bus from here. The Maestro stands.

'Sorry, go ahead to the party without me. I have to unearth this girl's paintings properly.'

IF I HADN'T MET YOU

The Maestro rushes off towards the bus stop.

I watch the Maestro's back as he walks away.

I think about the meaning of 'Maestro'. A master. A director. A leader. A teacher. A manager. An authority. A facilitator. An originator. I feel I understand why he likes being called 'Maestro'. He serves as the catalyst to inspire action, whether for an individual or for a cause. I'm sure countless rays of light never would have shone without meeting the Maestro.

But when I think about it, to a greater or lesser extent, maybe we all play that role for someone. We're all intertwined in each other's lives without even knowing it.

The sea breeze picks up, causing the cafe's parasols to sway.

A dog out on a walk nuzzles against Mark's feet. Its owner tugs at its leash.

'*Stop it, Jack!* I'm so sorry.'

'No worries,' Mark says and pets the dog. This is par for the course for him. Even when he's just minding his own business, dogs always seem drawn to him.

'Dogs really like you, Mark,' I say.

He nods. 'They do. I think I was a dog in my past life.'

At his confident declaration, as the idiom goes, I make my eyes black and white.

11

A Tricolour Promise

Purple

A handmade bookmark was enclosed in the airmail letter I had received from Maco in Japan. It featured a charming pink pressed flower, laminated for preservation, and tied with a white washi cord. Even as an Australian born and bred in Sydney, I know that flower. It was Maco who told me about it. It's the sakura, or cherry blossom, a flower Maco adores that signals the arrival of spring in Japan.

One lovely October weekend when Maco still lived in Sydney, I took her to my favourite place. It was a path lined with jacaranda trees, the branches of which created a magnificent purple arch. The fallen blossoms carpeting the ground were also a beautiful sight. The jacaranda is a symbol of Australia's spring.

'I love seeing the jacarandas here. This purple landscape always makes me think, *Ah, spring is here!*' I said.

Maco's eyes lit up, and she began speaking about the sakura. She told me how the Japanese also associate the blooming of cherry blossoms with the arrival of spring; that they, too, are often planted to line streets; that their delicate pink hue has a similar tone to the jacaranda's pale purple; and that, in Tokyo, they reach peak bloom in April.

It felt odd to me that April was considered spring. I wondered if Maco found it just as strange that spring in Australia was in October.

'Ah, I wish I could show you, Mary! I, too, have a favourite place where the sakura blooms,' said Maco.

I nodded. 'Yes. One day, I'll visit Tokyo in April to see the cherry blossoms.'

I didn't mean to say something for politeness' sake – it simply flowed out of me naturally. Maco looked at me with a breathless expression; then her face blossomed into a smile.

'That's a promise!'

Ten years ago, when Maco was still in high school, she came to live with my family for a year as an exchange student.

A TRICOLOUR PROMISE

I still clearly remember how I felt when I first met her. The moment I saw her, I thought, *How I've missed her.* As if awoken by an ancient memory, I felt myself – a self older than my current one – stir within me. It felt like I already possessed memories of her, but at the time, I didn't know what they were.

I was born with a heart condition. With the exception of gym class, my daily life was similar to that of other kids, but still, I tended to stay at home. Worried about my introversion, my parents began hosting exchange students, hoping to provide me with opportunities to socialize with girls my age.

Most of the Japanese girls we hosted were considerate of my condition and told me to take it easy, but they seemed unsure how to behave around me. They seemed hesitant to tell me stories about enjoying the outdoors with friends or about their excursions.

Maco, on the other hand, had no such barriers. She shared her experiences freely, adding wild gestures to dramatize her story. Even the most trivial discovery was relayed to me as if she had unearthed treasure. The time spent with Maco gave me much joy, like seeing life bloom in a barren desert.

She also took me out of the house, always making sure I didn't overexert myself. Gradually, I experienced the fresh air outside, found myself gazing at nature, and began to find pleasure in spending time in cafes. Maco, who was five years younger than me, should have been like a sweet little sister to me, but in reality, she was the one who was subtly guiding me forward.

Maco and I could talk endlessly. But, paradoxically, we could also spend hours in the same room, silently doing our own thing.

How many airmail letters were exchanged between us after Maco returned to Japan? Although we hadn't made any promises, my absolute certainty that a reply would always come kept me going through my otherwise rocky days.

Maco's English language skills continued to grow, and occasionally, I felt as though I was receiving letters from a native speaker. Since I mentioned that the delicate paper and the tricolour envelope of her first letter were so lovely, she never once strayed from that style. The only thing that changed was that she switched from writing in a ballpoint pen to the fountain pen I had gifted her.

We repeatedly expressed our desire to see each other again, yet it never happened. Maco went off to college and, after graduating, became a teacher at an English language school. Because of her class schedule, it was difficult for her to take extended holidays, and my unpredictable health condition prevented me from travelling abroad.

We'd not seen each other since Maco returned to Japan. But the regular letters between us never faltered. Even when email became commonplace, we continued to cherish the physical act of writing and receiving letters because, to me, the airmail letters that travelled across the ocean embodied Maco herself.

In June of last year, I fell ill. My chronic heart condition had worsened.

After about a month in hospital, my doctor said it would be challenging to continue to treat me at this facility. He said he would write a referral for me to transfer to a larger hospital in central Sydney with more advanced medical equipment. I shook my head.

The hospital where I was staying was in the suburbs, and from my window, I had a clear, expansive view of the sea. I loved that view. The spacious private room was comfortable, and I adored my attending physician and the nurses.

A few years ago, I'd been admitted to the hospital my doctor mentioned for about a week for tests. I remembered seeing only buildings from the windows, the harried staff and the reek of disinfectant. Even if it had top-notch medical equipment, I didn't want to return to such a stressful environment.

'If I'm to meet my end, I'd rather it be here.'

One day in July, I said so in a letter to Maco.

Since childhood, I have always believed that I wouldn't live a long life. Before I started elementary school, I remember going to hospital with my mother and being left to wait outside the examination room. I quietly peeked into the room and saw the doctor and my mother in hushed conversation. Even though I was the one who was sick, my mother, who was supposed to be healthy, wore a pained frown. I haven't been able to get that image out of my head.

From then, I became fearful of my own mortality. I formed a habit of expecting nothing but the worst so as not to get my hopes up.

When Maco received my letter, she called me at the hospital. It was the first time she'd done something like that. When I took the international phone call at the nurses' station, she pleaded with me to transfer immediately to a bigger hospital and to try my best to get better.

'Mary, have you forgotten the promise you made to me?'

Maco was crying into the receiver.

'What promise?'

I was sorry, but I had no idea what promise Maco was referring to.

'If you don't remember, it's fine. But I'll continue to look forward to it,' she said before hanging up.

Maco had sounded angry on the phone, and I was

worried she might now hate me. Yet, a week later, I received an unexpectedly cheerful letter from her. There was a brown stain, like a spill, on the edge of the first page with a speech bubble that read, 'Warm up with some hot chocolate!'

'If you love it at this current hospital, Mary, perhaps it's better for you to carry on your medical treatment there at your own pace instead of transferring elsewhere,' she wrote.

She had been adamantly against my staying. What changed her mind?

'Someone told me that "just being in a place you like can sometimes give you strength".'

When I read that line, I finally remembered my promise to Maco. To see the cherry blossoms in April in her favourite place.

I wrote back to her immediately.

'I'll get well by autumn, and I'll visit Japan. I'll see the cherry blossoms with you, Maco.'

But my condition gradually worsened. After detailed testing at the end of the year, it was determined that I required major surgery. If it went well, I might have a chance at a normal life, but the risks were substantial. The doctor said the chances were fifty–fifty. If I were to undergo the surgery, I would need to prepare myself for the possibility that I might not wake up from it.

I was terrified. But if I had a 50 per cent chance of recovery, I was willing to gamble on it. I would undergo surgery and regain my health so I could see the cherry blossoms with Maco. I'd promised that I would.

During surgery, under the haze of anaesthesia, I had a blurry vision.

How long ago was it? Two girls huddled together in a small, rural town in Australia. An older sister gently giving freshly gathered flowers to her frail younger sister lying in bed. The contours of the fuzzy memory gradually sharpened.

The sickly little sister – that was me. The older sister watching over her – that was Maco. We were sisters in a distant past life.

Me in my past life was terrified of dying and lived in fear. Me in my current life was no different. To fear death and to fear life were the same thing.

'These flowers are blooming all over the plaza. They're gorgeous. We have to go see them together,' said my sister by my bedside that day.

I nodded, but I doubted it would be possible. It would take two hours by foot to get to the plaza. It was too far a distance for me.

Suddenly, I was bathed in a brilliant light.

It was a sensation I'd experienced before. In my

A TRICOLOUR PROMISE

past life, a young me had reached out to the light without hesitation.

My sister was calling out to me.

But I didn't answer her. I was weak. To continue living in pain was too exhausting.

It would be better if it just ended.

I'm sorry I couldn't see the flowers with you, sister.

The life I'd given up at that moment.

The memory of my past life that vanished.

It was undoubtedly going to be the same. Even if I were reborn, I'd forget everything again.

. . .

'Mary!'

I pull back my hand from the light with a start.

'Mary, have you forgotten? Our promise? I've been looking forward to it.'

Maco was crying.

Such a sensitive soul. She was so much stronger than me, but she'd tear up over something as trivial as a flower wilting. Maco, who excitedly re-enacted the musical she'd seen at the Opera House.

You were wide-eyed in amazement, marvelling at the size of the Australian beef on the barbecue grill. I couldn't swim in the ocean, so you kept me company on the beach under the parasol, where we ate fish and chips together. At night, we stood side by side on the veranda and searched for the Southern Cross constellation in the sky.

On Maco's last night in Sydney, we fell asleep in my bed, holding hands, our heads touching. Maco was, as expected, crying, wishing the next day wouldn't come. I cried, too.

Airmail from Maco. Though apart, we exchanged warm letters that connected our separate worlds. I have a whole box of them.

Maco, thank you for coming to Sydney. For meeting me.

I remember our first meeting vividly.

The smiling face of Maco that I'd missed.

. . . missed?

That's right.

In that moment, I had remembered that I knew her. My memory from my past life hadn't been erased – what was necessary had remained. This was so I could instantly recognize she was someone important. So I could make good on the promise I had broken. I've been given another chance.

'Mary!'

I could hear Maco calling out to me.

This time, I responded.

'Maco!'

I would live.

In this lifetime, I would live fully.

A TRICOLOUR PROMISE

Not because we were sisters in our past lives. We would live our present selves.

After the surgery, I woke. A new me was waiting.

Under the autumn sky of April, I boarded a plane from Sydney Airport.

The remarkable speed of my recovery had surprised my doctor but not me. My body had made sure to heal in time for the cherry blossoms. Jacarandas bloomed all spring, but the sakura's bloom lasted only a few days, so I couldn't waste time.

It's my first time visiting Tokyo. Maco and I are reunited after a decade. Together, we view the cherry blossoms in full bloom along the river.

At the riverbank bustling with cherry blossom viewers, I tell Maco, 'It's your turn to come to Sydney next to see the jacarandas with me.'

Maco smiles and nods vigorously, her chestnut hair swaying.

'It's a promise!'

We live in ignorance of what the next second holds. There are things beyond our control that come to us unbidden. In those moments, anxieties that multiply endlessly cause us to imagine fearful scenarios. Even though these are stories of our own fabrication, we are threatened by them as if they were immutable futures handed down to us by someone.

But in reality, none of that exists. The only things that I know exist for certain, here and now, are the breathing me, the smiling Maco, and the blooming cherry blossoms.

The petals dance on the water's surface as they drift away.

I'll keep living, looking forward to the day our promise comes true. When Maco comes to Sydney, and we see the jacarandas again, we'll make a new promise.

With that vow in my heart, I gaze dreamily at the cherry blossoms carried away by the river's current.

12

A Love Letter

White

I'm in my usual seat today, writing you a letter.

As I sip on the hot chocolate you just brought me, I'm going to take my time to tell you how I feel.

A year and a half has passed since I began coming to this Marble Cafe. I don't mind the predictable comfort of chain coffee shops, but I love the relaxed, comforting atmosphere of this one-of-a-kind cafe.

I also enjoy the rotating artwork on the walls. The pastel piece, with its many overlapping green circles, which has been up since last week, gives me this wonderful nostalgic feeling of retracing a distant memory.

You don't wear a name badge, and since you're the only one working at the cafe with no other staff to call out to you, I don't know your real name. I only know that you might be a few years younger than me and that you're a hard worker.

But it's fine. Ever since my first visit to this cafe, I've secretly given you a name.

It was a snowy winter's day. While shopping at the general store along the river, I noticed, for the first time, a glowing lamp behind the large trees across the bridge. Perhaps I'd not seen it until then because I was usually distracted by the rows of cherry blossom trees. Now stripped of their flowers and leaves, the Marble Cafe revealed itself. In search of warmth amid the biting cold, I crossed the bridge.

The cafe was so warm and peaceful that it almost brought tears to my eyes. A lush ficus plant looked comfortable standing by the entrance. The simple, raw wood tables and chairs seemed eager to welcome guests.

I sat in a corner by the window and let out a sigh of relief. My numb hands, frozen cheeks and ears were thawing, and my body felt like it was unwinding itself.

A little boy with a mushroom haircut and his young father sat at the next table. The boy held a model plane over his head, swooshing it in the air and laughing with pure joy. It seemed they had arrived a little before me and were waiting for their order.

I opened the menu and was deciding between the café au lait and Earl Grey tea when you brought the drinks to the neighbouring table.

A LOVE LETTER

'Ah! It's Takumi's hot chocolate!' the boy exclaimed happily. The way the boy said 'hot chocolate' was so adorable I couldn't help but look his way.

You first gave his father his coffee, then placed the hot chocolate before Takumi.

'Here's your hot chocolate. Please be careful, as it's hot,' you cautioned Takumi with a smile.

If you'd simply said, 'Careful, it's hot,' you'd have come across as a polite server. But in your voice, there was a clear sense of respect and pride in your work, and it captured my heart. You treated the boy, probably still in kindergarten, with such sincerity, as if he were any other important customer. And the incredibly gentle way you said 'hot chocolate'.

He's the real deal. That's what I thought.

You weren't following some conventional manual; it was genuine care.

When you left their table, I called you over and placed my order.

'I'll have a hot chocolate, please.'

You repeated back my order with a warm smile. 'Yes, a hot chocolate.'

The 'hot chocolate' that spilled from your lips again was slightly more bitter than the one you gave Takumi, but it had a faint sweetness, and I desperately suppressed a grin.

Meeting you made me realize something for the

first time: there's not just 'love at first sight' but 'love at first voice'.

And that's when I decided on your name.

Mr Hot Chocolate.

I've been calling you that in my heart ever since.

This is where I always write my letters to my friend in Sydney.

I lived there for a year as an exchange student when I was in high school. Mary is the only child of the host family.

I'd thought I was good at English, but living among native speakers, I realized that my language skills were inadequate. But curiously, Mary and I could understand each other with just a few words. At times, a glance was enough to convey our feelings.

Even between Japanese people who speak the same language, there are times when we misunderstand each other or don't understand what the other is thinking. Maybe that's what 'miscommunication' actually is.

To this point, Mary was someone with whom I could communicate well. Even when she used words I didn't know, I could understand her without issue. Conversely, when I stumbled over my English, she could pick up on exactly what I wanted to say. Before I knew it, English spilled from my lips

without my trying, as if I was 'remembering' words I'd used before. It felt as if I was 'returning' to being an easy-going Australian person who spoke English as their native tongue, and I started to believe it. But this magic didn't happen when I was with others, so I still needed to study hard to properly learn English.

Writing to her from Japan is, in a sense, a kind of therapy for my spirit. It allows me to return to my true self amid the chaos of daily life and move forward anew. When I discovered Marble Cafe, I thought I'd found the perfect place to write letters. It was a special space where I could be myself and write to Mary.

Mary and I rarely argued, but once, we had a quarrel-like exchange over the phone. It was last year when she was admitted to hospital with a life-threatening illness.

Despite being advised by the doctor to transfer to a larger hospital, she refused, saying, 'I like it here.' I selfishly pushed her to transfer and told her she needed to do everything she could to get better. I was so scared of losing my dear friend I might have lost sight of her perspective.

Downhearted, I came to the cafe for your hot chocolate, but my favourite spot was occupied. I resigned myself to another table and was lost in thought for a while when you suddenly spoke to me. 'The table's free. It's your usual spot. Just being in a place you like can sometimes give you strength.'

Mr Hot Chocolate, I bet you have no idea how surprised, happy and relieved I felt at that moment. Before I knew it, you'd wiped down my usual table, and it sparkled as if it were meant just for me.

Just being in a place you like can sometimes give you strength. I knew this was true. I finally understood that being somewhere she felt comfortable was the best treatment for Mary. I knew I was much happier here than at a fancy restaurant with no special meaning to me.

The reason why I always pick this table is because it feels cosy in the corner, I can see my beloved cherry blossoms from the window and it's the spot where I fell for you on that snowy day.

This table always feels welcoming and brings back memories of that day with remarkable vividness. I sit here, covertly watching you, looking so content at work. I've mastered the art of keeping you within my peripheral vision without our eyes meeting. Because if they do, you, ever so diligent, will probably rush over to ask if I need anything. And if that happens, I may blurt out, *I love you*.

Mary overcame her illness, recovered in the blink of an eye and, yesterday, she came to visit me in Tokyo.

A LOVE LETTER

We stood side by side and observed the cherry blossoms by the river. We also promised that I'd visit Sydney next.

There are many things I want to do that I haven't accomplished yet. With a little effort, they're probably within reach.

To chat with a person I like, while I observe scenery I like, at a place I like.

Until now, I've been holding back on such an important wish.

However, if you don't go for it when the inclination arises, you might stay stuck for ever. Worse, your wishes and desires might even fade away with your feelings.

I think of you often as I watch the river flow under the row of cherry blossom trees.

I always come to the Marble Cafe at three o'clock on Thursdays, my day off.

Same table. Same order.

Just watching you from here is enough for me.

Just exchanging the words 'Can I have a hot chocolate, please?' with you is enough for me.

But I've started wanting to break out from my usual routine.

From now on, I want to witness the scattering pink petals, the fresh green of young leaves, the deep red of autumn leaves, and the pure white of snow with you.

I want to tell you about my life. And I want you to tell me about yours. I want to hear everything – your dreams that seem light-years away and events so tiny they fit in the palm of your hand.

So, Mr Hot Chocolate.

Won't you remove your apron and go out with me sometime?

This letter has got quite long. I'm about to finish my first love letter, seal it and give it to you.

And I'll add a little something with a smile: 'Please be careful, as it's hot.'

Do you need more books by Michiko Aoyama?
Now read the fabulous, irresistible sequel

MATCHA ON MONDAY

Translated from the Japanese by E. Madison Shimoda

I

Matcha on Monday

月曜日の抹茶カフェ

[January • Tokyo]

I press my hands together and pray for something good to happen, but where is my prayer actually going?

Well, I'm at a Shinto shrine, so it's headed to a Shinto god. Probably.

But where did the gods reside? On the other side of this offertory box? Up in the sky? Or . . .?

It's almost the middle of the month, but since this is my first shrine visit of the year, it's essentially my hatsumode – my 'first prayer' for the new year.

I work at a mobile phone store in a shopping mall. The mall stayed open during the New Year's holiday, so we didn't get any time off. Although they tried to schedule us in short, rotating shifts, employees like me, who are single, often yielded longer breaks to those with families and ended up taking on extra shifts ourselves.

When I didn't have time to help prepare the New

Year Osechi meal, my parents complained, saying, 'Miho, you're already twenty-six.' But I'm currently in my prime working years, so I hope they cut me some slack. Ever since I was a child, I've loved all things mechanical, so I enjoy working with mobile phones.

But the January shift schedule was different from usual, and having misread it, I showed up for an early shift today, even though it was my day off.

Bummer. I could've stayed up late last night and slept in.

I didn't feel like going home straight away, so I took a stroll around the mall. There are days when nothing goes right. I dropped by a clothing store to buy a down jacket I'd had my eye on, but it was sold out. Trying to shake off that disappointment, I went into a fast-food place, but then spilled the ketchup for my fries and got it on the sleeve of my sweater. I went to the bathroom to try to rinse off the ketchup, only to realize I'd forgotten my handkerchief.

I'm not exactly the lucky type to begin with, but today feels especially jinxed. Maybe it's because I haven't gone for my first prayer this year. It's a bit of a walk from the mall to the shrine, but I thought I should pay it a visit. Maybe I could get cleansed of my bad luck while I was at it.

That was what I was thinking about as I offered

my prayers at the shrine when the Marble Cafe suddenly came to mind.

Straight down the street along the river near the shrine, you'll find a small coffee shop where the row of cherry blossom trees ends. It's a cosy place managed by a lovely young man, and the interior design is incredibly stylish. And, of course, the coffee and tea are delicious. I only go occasionally when I have an early shift, but it's a particular favourite of mine. On a day as unlucky as this, I should go to my favourite place to lift my spirits.

As I walk, I glance sideways at the cluster of cherry blossom trees with their bare boughs devoid of blooms and leaves.

My breath warms the red checked scarf around my mouth. My hands in my pockets are numb from the cold.

From the shadows of the trees, the Marble Cafe's awning emerges. *I want to go inside quickly and warm up.* I stop in my tracks.

Today is Monday. Marble Cafe is closed on Mondays.

Just my luck. If only I'd remembered sooner, I wouldn't have walked all the way here. Only to remember as I'm about to arrive . . .

I let out a loud sigh.

Just when I'm about to turn around, the cafe door opens.

I glance over. A woman with a pixie cut comes out and walks towards me. She looks as if she's older than me. Her hair, dyed an ash brown, is glossy.

'Excuse me,' I call out as she passes me. The woman turns her slender eyes my way. 'Isn't Marble Cafe closed today?'

'It's closed, but it's open. Why don't you check it out?'

A husky voice, pleasing to the ear. As she strides away, I think, *Wow, how cool is she?*

As advised, I walk up to the front of the cafe and peer through the window. People are scattered here and there at both the counter and the tables.

I'm about to reach for the doorknob when my eyes pause on the shop sign. White masking tape covers the 'rble' of Marble Cafe, and the letters 'tcha' in black marker are written over it. Matcha Cafe.

Matcha Cafe? Is this a joke?

I tilt my head at the sign, which feels a little too rough for a rebrand. Just then, the door swings open and a small-framed man sticks his head out. 'Please come in.'

I notice the large mole on his forehead and recall seeing him at the cafe before. The friendly manager referred to him as Maestro. But he had been seated at the counter reading the sports pages and didn't appear to work there.

MATCHA ON MONDAY

The man with the mole, whom we'll call the Maestro, said, 'We're a matcha cafe just for today. If you don't dislike matcha, please come in.'

I enter the cafe, feeling saved.

Inside, there's a couple seated at a table at the back and a man dressed in a navy-blue kimono standing behind the counter. I take a seat at the table near the counter and shrug off my coat.

I finally feel relief wash over me. My body craves a milky green matcha latte.

'Welcome.'

The man in the kimono places a glass of water on the table and hands me the menu. It is written in brush on Japanese paper mounted on cardboard and reads:

Koicha (dark tea) 1,200 yen
Usucha (light tea) 700 yen
Both come with traditional confections.

I'm stumped.

This isn't your typical matcha latte or matcha pudding kind of situation. It's rather authentic.

'. . . Um, is this all?'

'It is.'

Even though the man has come to take my order, he's looking off into the distance with a blank face.

He has a defined jaw and a slender nose. He appears about five years older than me. He seems completely at ease in traditional Japanese attire and has the air of a pretentious young gentleman.

He remains turned away from me as he waits for my answer. I drop my gaze to the menu. If there's no pudding, I don't mind having Japanese sweets. I don't know the difference between koicha and usucha, but the pricier one must be tastier. I just came from my hatsumode, so why not splurge a little in the spirit of the New Year's good luck prayer?

'The koicha, please.'

When I look up from the menu, our eyes meet, but the young gentleman turns his face away with surprising speed. '*Koicha*, then,' he mumbles, and hurries over to the counter.

He didn't have to be *that* repulsed. His obvious contempt stings, and I feel disheartened. I shouldn't have come. I look around the cafe.

The Maestro is seated at the counter, reading the sports pages. Just as he was when I last saw him.

The couple are quietly conversing. At a glance, they seem to be in their late thirties. Simple bands adorn their ring fingers. A married couple, probably.

I feel envious – a stable, trusting relationship.

As I sit there, gazing dreamily at the happy couple, the Maestro turns to me. 'You dropped your scarf.'

I look down and find the scarf I draped over my lap lying limp on the floor. As I pick it up, the Maestro asks me a question.

'Do you come to our cafe often?'

Our cafe. He must be the owner, after all.

'Every now and then. I actually came by mistake today – I know the cafe's usually closed on Monday. I didn't know you did things like this, a one-day-only matcha cafe.'

'Yes, we sometimes hold events on our days off or after hours.'

I had no idea. Marble Cafe is such a charming place, yet it doesn't advertise or seem to have an online presence.

'Shouldn't you promote these events on your website or on social media? Posting details could bring in more customers.'

The corners of the Maestro's lips turn up, and he lets out a *hmph* through his nose.

'It's more fun when people end up here by chance or somehow find themselves here – just like you did – don't you think?'

'You mean by fate?'

'I suppose so,' he says and raises a forefinger. 'Whether it's people or objects, a single encounter suggests it was meant to be. Fate is something like a seed, you see. Even if it's small or plain, it can blossom into a beautiful flower or bear delicious fruit – things you could never have imagined when it was just a seed.'

The jacket that sold out before I could buy it comes to mind, and I counter, 'But aren't there times when you do meet, but it's just a one-off, and things end before they have a chance to grow?'

'That doesn't mean it wasn't fate; you were fated to meet just once. It's like eating a sunflower seed. The experience becomes part of you, and in some way it might lead to something else down the road.'

Sunflower seeds. I tilt my head. *I've never eaten one before*.

The Maestro chuckles.

'Well, today's more for fun than profit. So it really doesn't matter to me how many customers show up. Welcome to Monday's matcha cafe!'

Is it really just for fun?

As I ponder this, the young gentleman arrives with a black lacquered tray.

'Thank you for waiting. Here is your koicha. The wagashi sweet is kan bontan, or winter peony.'

There's a hint of the west in his intonation. I can tell he's from the Kansai region.

The wagashi named 'winter peony' is a beautiful pink neri-kiri, a confection made from sweetened

white bean paste and glutinous rice flour. A yellow stamen peeks out from the centre of frill-like folds.

'How lovely. Braving the bitter cold while trying to bloom with strength – how truly wonderful,' says the Maestro, before turning back to the counter and flipping through his newspaper.

The couple stand up, and the young gentleman heads to the cash register. The woman notices the packs of tea displayed by the register and buys one. When they've gone, leaving just the three of us at the cafe, I take a moment to admire the delicate floral wagashi.

And the koicha that sits beside it. As its name suggests, it is a very dark green. When I lift the teacup with both hands, it feels thick like paint.

How delicious this is going to be, I think, but the moment I take a sip, I reflexively pull the cup away from my lips.

'Buh-eh!' A strange noise slips out before I can stop it. It wasn't very loud, but it echoed strangely in the silent cafe.

The tea is intense. It's not just bitter or tart. It has an unfamiliar flavour with a harsh edge that I can't even put into words.

The Maestro laughs. 'You're supposed to eat the sweets first.'

I quickly slice the wagashi in half and stuff it into

my mouth. I had intended to eat it more gracefully, but it can't be helped.

After sweetening my palate with the wagashi, I give the drink another try. It seems more tolerable this time, and I believe I can better appreciate the complexity of this flavour . . . but it's still challenging. I find myself blinking in astonishment. *What kind of penance is this?* Yet, given the cost of 1,200 yen, I'm reluctant to abandon it.

As I glug my glass of water, a ringtone sounds from the counter. The young gentleman grabs his mobile phone.

'Uhh? Huh?' He impatiently taps his phone screen.

Without thinking, I say, 'You just need to swipe up.'

'Swipe?' He looks at me.

'Keep your finger on the screen and slide it upward.'

He looks relieved that he has managed to answer the call before the caller hung up. 'Yeah . . . no, I didn't call you,' he says into the phone.

I look away. With the last piece of the wagashi still in my mouth, I desperately gulp down the last of the koicha.

I chose the pricier option to lift my spirits, yet here I am. Just how unlucky am I today?

As the young gentleman ends his call, the Maestro asks him, 'Your father?'

'Yes. Apparently this thing called him on its own, so he was calling me back.' He points at his phone with a look of contempt. 'Two weeks ago, I switched to this from my dumbphone. It keeps nagging me with "updates", and if I follow its instructions, the apps change and become harder to navigate. And I thought I'd bought a brand-new, top-of-the-range model . . .'

Unable to contain myself any longer, I say, 'The thing about smartphones is that they're not a fully finished product from start to end.'

The young gentleman and Maestro both turn to look at me.

'I work with smartphones, and I feel this every day: the world of smartphones is constantly evolving – new viruses will pop up, network stability will fluctuate, and society's needs change. The smartphone needs to make constant minor updates to keep up with the ever-changing environment.'

The Maestro nods with a thoughtful 'Hmm.'

Encouraged, I continue.

'Unfortunately, sometimes updates introduce bugs. But small setbacks like that make smartphones better in the long run. I think it's fantastic that without changing its physical form, it can try new things or expand its capabilities. It almost feels like they're alive. I can't help but find them endearing!'

As soon as I finish, I clap my hand to my mouth.

I've rambled. This always happens when I start talking about smartphones. It's a bad habit of mine.

The young gentleman lowers his gaze and asks, 'Would you care for some ousu?'

'Ousu?'

'I'm referring to usucha – light matcha, the frothy matcha most people are familiar with. It's easy to drink, I believe. It'll be on the house as a thank you for teaching me how to answer my phone.'

The Maestro then turns to me and says, 'Want to watch the tea being made?'

'Can I? I'd love to watch!'

As I lean forward, the young gentleman gives a slight nod. The Maestro chuckles as he folds away his newspaper.

'You know, as they say, "Good vibes and good luck go hand in hand."'

'Whose quote is that?'

'Mine,' the Maestro replies as he goes to the magazine rack next to the cash register, newspaper in hand. He is an elusive man.

A few moments later, the young gentleman returns to my table with a tray and teapot and places them before me. On the tray are a teacup, a bamboo whisk and teaspoon, and a strainer.

The empty teacup is apparently pre-warmed. The ends of the whisk are slightly damp.

MATCHA ON MONDAY

'Now, I'll begin.'

First, the young gentleman puts one and a half scoops of matcha tea powder in the strainer using the bamboo teaspoon, which resembles an oversized earpick. He then uses the back of the spoon to break up any clumps. Once the matcha is smooth and fine in the teacup, he gently pours hot water over it and sets the whisk in place.

'Move the whisk forward, backward, and then forward again – as if you were writing an M.'

'M? Like the letter from the English alphabet?'

'Yes.'

The young gentleman appears perplexed by my query. I pose another question.

'How did people explain this before the English alphabet was known? Like how did the sixteenth-century tea-master Sen no Rikyū explain it?'

The young gentleman bursts into laughter.

'I wonder. I've never thought about it.'

Huh.

I had no idea this guy had such an adorable smile. He ought to show it more often.

A warm, gooey sweetness, like ice cream melting deep in my chest, spreads through me. *Woah. What is this feeling?*

The young gentleman moves the whisk in swift zigzags, then gently strokes the surface of the tea as if to pop the large bubbles. After that, he gives it one more intense whisk.

'Finally, draw the letter の, and remove the whisk slowly.'

After lifting the whisk straight up from the centre of the cup, the young gentleman adds, 'Maybe even Sen no Rikyū mentioned the の shape.'

He finally meets my gaze. This time, it's me who can't look directly at him, and my eyes dart around.

The young gentleman goes back to the counter once and returns with a plate of wagashi. 'This is a "snow rabbit",' he says, placing it on the tray. It's an adorable little white mochi confection that looks as if it might be hopping around on a snowy mountain.

After slowly savouring the wagashi, I take a sip of the usucha. It's delicious. The sophisticated sweetness of the confection layers gently with the fragrant aroma of the tea. Enjoying them in this order, as suggested, enhances their flavours.

Finally, my heart settles and I let out a sigh of relief.

'I'm so grateful for your extra service. I have such bad luck. It feels like only unlucky things ever happen to me. Just one thing after another today.'

I list the things that have or haven't happened to me during the day.

The young gentleman, listening patiently, tilts his head.

'Rather than being unlucky, maybe you're . . .'

'Hmm?'

'. . . just clumsy?'

He looks deadly serious. I thought we had warmed up to each other a little, so it feels like I've been pricked with a needle. I guess he really doesn't like me after all. But then he continues.

'You're not unlucky at all. You have a job you can speak passionately about – that alone makes you incredibly lucky. The smartphone must feel happy to be cared for and cherished by you.'

. . . The smartphone . . . happy?

I never thought about it that way before. The idea that a smartphone might somehow feel my passion and be happy – it makes me feel acknowledged and rewarded.

And, yeah, I'm just clumsy. I'm not unlucky. The laughter that wells up inside me is accompanied by a few tears. I'm happy. Very happy.

I rummage through my bag looking for something to wipe my cheeks. Oh, right, I left my handkerchief in the bathroom today.

Then, something silently materializes before me: a neatly folded navy hand towel. The young gentleman is facing away from me, his expression sullen. When I look closely, I notice that his ears are red.

'Um, thank you very much.'

When I take the towel from him, the young gentleman says to the Maestro, 'I'm going to take out the trash,' and leaves.

In the corner of the towel, the character 吉, meaning 'luck', is embroidered in white thread. What is this? Some kind of good-luck charm?

'Oh, he's using that! I gave that to him as a gift,' says the Maestro, who, having finished the paper, is now reading a weekly magazine. 'That's his name embroidered there. 吉 is the first character of his name: 吉平, Kippei. A lucky name, don't you think? He's the only child of a tea dealer called Fukui-do. Fukui means 'where fortune resides'. Kippei Fukui – it's a name wrapped up in good fortune.'

So his name is Kippei.

Forgetting my handkerchief turned out to be a good thing.

I let my mind wander.

If I had been able to buy that jacket, I might have gone straight home. And if I hadn't mistaken today for a workday, I wouldn't have come here. In a way, it's my clumsiness that brought me to the matcha cafe. *I must be incredibly lucky.*

Will I see him again if I come here?

'When are you doing a matcha cafe again?' I ask the Maestro.

'Oh, it's just for today. Fukui-do is based in Kyoto,

you see. Kippei came to Tokyo for the first time to attend a meeting on his father's behalf – but he'll be heading back tomorrow.'

Right . . . I guess I won't be seeing him again.
See? I'm not lucky, after all.

Just as I'm beginning to feel disappointed, I reconsider.

If I want to see him again, I simply need to act in a way that will make it happen. The fact that I came here means I've been given the seed for our connection. I just have to do my best to nurture it.

I pretend to rest my chin in my hands, softly pressing my palms together beneath my jaw.

May I meet Kippei once more. May good things come my way. As I press my hands tightly together, I channel my prayers into the warmth of my body.

That's right – prayers are meant to be made into these hands.

'But you know,' says the Maestro, flipping the pages of his magazine, 'they're opening a Tokyo branch, and he's going to manage it. He's moving here on his own in the spring.'

The prayer I made into my palms sprouts with a pop. I squeeze my hands.

I'm okay. I'm incredibly lucky.

Michiko Aoyama was born in 1970 in Aichi Prefecture, Honshu, Japan. She is the author of the multi-million-copy bestselling *What You Are Looking For is in the Library*, which was a *Time* Book of the Year, a *Times* bestseller and a *New York Times* Book of the Month. Her latest novel to be translated into English, *Hot Chocolate on Thursday*, is her debut, which tells of the Marble Cafe, a tiny community cafe in Tokyo, and is set partly in Japan and partly in Sydney, Australia. It is a companion read to *Matcha on Monday*, coming soon in translation. Another book available in English by Aoyama is the international bestseller *The Healing Hippo of Hinode Park*. Aoyama lives in Yokohama, Japan.